Further Endorsements for
Josie

"Let me begin by saying how much I enjoyed it!...I, at least, was totally entranced by the characters and their fate! As a historian, I also think that Josie's story is important and well worth telling. Her fate, while not entirely typical in all its specifics, *is* representative of the fate of so many innocent victims of national discrimination. Her story, which so captures the imagination, forces the reader to reevaluate abuses long ignored and even tolerated simply because they were perpetrated against an accepted enemy—in this case, the Germans. At the same time, the authors carefully avoided the common error of blaming (in this case) all Serbs for the crimes committed by only a few."

—*Carol Lilly, PhD (Yale), Professor and Director of International Studies Program. Eastern Europe, Russian, and Soviet History, University of Nebraska at Kearney; Author of "Problems of Persuasion: Communist Agitation and Propaganda in Post-War Yugoslavia, 1944–1948"*

"Josie's, *Opa's* remarks, 'We are no better than slaves.' Apparently, to *Opa*, slavery was the most fitting analogy for the treatment of the ethnic Germans in Yugoslavia. One could argue, however, that slavery is too mild an analogy for the horrors that befell millions of East Central European Germans between 1944 and 1950. Slave masters usually want to protect their investment. These Germans, however, were expendable. The fewer of them that survived, the less complicated their eventual resettlement and integration. Susan Lowe and Diane Iverson's book contributes to the slowly growing body of literature on the fate of this largely ignored population. The authors' lens is on the interrupted childhood of their close relative, Josie Trollmann. As we celebrate her survival we must above all, validate her trauma and loss. Regardless of the audience *Josie* targets, it is an informative, accessible and necessary read for anyone."

—*Brigitte Neary, PhD (Duke University), Professor of Sociology, Criminal Justice, and Women's Studies, University of South Carolina Upstate; author of "Voices of Loss: German Women Recount Their Expulsion From East-Central Europe, 1944-1950. Rockport, Maine: Picton Press, 2002 (with Holle Schneider-Ricks)"*

Josie

Josie

A STORY OF FAITH AND SURVIVAL

• • •

Susan Lowe and Diane Iverson

Illustrated by Diane Iverson

ISBN: 1517061008
ISBN 13: 9781517061005
Library of Congress Control Number: 2015916353
CreateSpace Independent Publishing Platform
North Charleston, South Carolina

Dedication

• • •

In loving memory of my mother, Josie.
Susan Lowe

In memory of all innocent victims of war.
Diane Iverson

Table of Contents

Foreword

• • •

THIS IS A TRUE STORY. As a young Fulbright fellow in Germany, I spent weeks in the German Federal Archives in Koblenz, plunging through thousands of reports of expellees from East Prussia, Pomerania, Silesia, East Brandenburg, Bohemia, Moravia, Carpathia, Hungary, Romania, and Yugoslavia. Fifteen million human beings were expelled—and they were made to pay collectively for the crimes of the Nazis. At the Nuremberg trials, the US chief prosecutor Robert Jackson had said that the guilty would be punished, not the innocent! Indeed, the whole idea of Nuremberg was to punish the political and military leaders who unleashed the war and brought untold suffering to many populations, including the Germans of Germany and the ethnic Germans of Yugoslavia.

I interviewed hundreds of *Vertriebene* (expellees) with similar experiences. The fifteen million *Vertriebene* had not been war profiteers. They had already suffered the privations of war, the bombardment of their cities and towns, and the loss of loved ones in the armed forces. At the end of hostilities, civilian populations are supposed to return to their lives, but this was not the case with the vanquished Germans. In violation of general principles of international law, in breach of specific provisions of the Hague Conventions and the Regulations on Land Warfare (1907), they were subjected to eviction from their homes, confiscation of their private property, internment for years, deportation to slave labor, and ultimately to permanent expulsion and loss of their homeland. Not less than two million persons perished as a consequence of massacres, extrajudicial executions, forced labor, exhaustion, malnutrition, disease—and the cumulative effects of their expulsion. Indeed, even after reaching relative safety in the bombed-out cities in Western Germany, these poor expellees continued dying because of lack of shelter and food.

An incredible level of hate prevailed against the entire German population. The war did not end for them, because the victors were intent on implementing the Roman practice of *vae victis* (woe to the vanquished) instead of the maxim of the Peace of Westphalia: *pax optima rerum* (peace is the highest good). Sixty-four years after the Second World War these prejudices and resentments persist, notwithstanding the Universal Declaration of Human Rights, notwithstanding article twenty of the International Covenant on Civil and Political Rights, which prohibits incitement to racial hatred. Alas, the media, television, Hollywood, and even schoolbooks all are guilty of keeping the hatred alive.

This historical novel reminds us that injustice is everywhere, that innocent people are victimized for no reason, and that stereotypes persist. We observe that when the underdog becomes top dog, he behaves as every top dog ever does. The new top dog preys on his victim. The Nazis committed awful crimes against Jews, Poles, Czechs, Russians, and Yugoslavs, but at the end of the war the victims turned victimizers, and millions of totally innocent people were made to suffer—people like Trollmann *Opa*, Andreas, and Josie. Alas, the vicious circle of injustice continues until someone decides to break the chain. The German expellees did so when they adopted the Charter of the Expellees in August 1950, in which they permanently renounced revenge and pledged themselves to advance the right to one's homeland only and exclusively by peaceful means.

May this book help some twenty-first-century readers reassess the Second World War and its aftermath—may it help them understand the horrors of Vietnam, Iraq, and Afghanistan. There are thousands of stories like Josie's, and the human dignity of these victims is the same as the human dignity of Anne Frank and of millions of other anonymous victims in Poland, Russia, Vietnam, Cambodia, Afghanistan, and Iraq. As the first UN high commissioner for human rights, José Ayala-Lasso, told the German expellees in Frankfurt on May 28, 1995:

"I submit that if in the years following the Second World War the States had reflected more on the implications of the enforced flight and the expulsion of the Germans, today's demographic catastrophes, particularly those referred to as 'ethnic cleansing,' would, perhaps, not have occurred to the same extent...

"There is no doubt that during the Nazi occupation the peoples of Central and Eastern Europe suffered enormous injustices that cannot be forgotten. Accordingly they had a legitimate claim for reparation. However, legitimate claims ought not to be enforced through collective punishment on the basis of general discrimination and without a determination of personal guilt. In the Nuremberg and Tokyo trials the crucial principle of personal responsibility for crimes was wisely applied. It is worthwhile to reread the Nuremberg protocols and judgment.

"Our goal remains the universal recognition of human rights, which are based on the principle of the equality of all human beings. Indeed, all victims of war and injustice deserve our respect and compassion, since every individual human life is precious. It is our duty to continue our endeavors in the name of the *dignitas humana.*"

Alfred de Zayas, JD (Harvard), PhD (Göttingen), UN Independent Expert on the Promotion of a Democratic and Equitable International Order since 2012, Professor of International Law at the Geneva School of Diplomacy, Retired Senior Lawyer with the UN High Commissioner for Human Rights, Former Secretary of the UN Human Rights Committee, President of the Swiss P.E.N. Club

Historical Background

• • •

THE TROLLMANN FAMILY HAD LIVED peacefully among their neighbors, in the small village of Glogon, for seven generations. In the 1700s Josie Trollmann's ancestors had traveled from Germany, sailing down the Danube River to settle in Austria-Hungary. The family immigrated during the Maria Theresian colonization, which occurred from 1744 to 1772. They came at the invitation of the Habsburg dynasty, along with thousands of other German immigrant families. Most of these families were of the Catholic faith. Together, they established villages, built churches, drained swamps, and developed farmland along the Danube as loyal citizens of their new country.

At the end of World War I, Austria-Hungary was dissolved, and the land was divided among Hungary, Romania, and a new Yugoslavia. What had been one large, united ethnic-German population became minority populations in each of these three countries. Glogon, the village where Josie's ancestors had lived since they immigrated, became part of Yugoslavia.

During World War II, Hitler's Nazi German forces occupied Yugoslavia. Their occupation lasted for three years, from 1941 to 1944. The Nazis committed many inexcusable war crimes. There was intense suffering throughout Europe, and Yugoslavia was no exception.

Most ethnic-German men in the region did not willingly join Nazi forces. Ninety percent of the Yugoslavian Nazi military division was conscripted "on penalty of death." Josie's father was one of those men forced into the Seventh SS Mountain Division, Prinz Eugen, against his will.

Communist Russian soldiers and Tito's partisans fought the Nazi Germans, and in 1944 they took control of Yugoslavia. Many Yugoslavs of German origin fled with the retreating German army in 1944, fearing what the Russians might do to them. Others, like Josie's family, considered themselves to be loyal Yugoslav citizens and remained in the only homes they had ever known. That was a fatal decision for many innocent people, and the beginning of a reign of terror for the rest.

So it was that in 1944, the same year that Anne Frank and her family were tragically captured and imprisoned by the Nazis in the Netherlands, Josie and her family were captured and imprisoned or sent into forced labor by the Communists.

There was little sympathy for the plight of families like Josie's because hatred of Germans was so raw for Hitler's victims. From 1944 to 1949 Yugoslavia's ethnic Germans lost their homeland, their rights as citizens, and all their possessions. They were now seen as enemies of the state. Many lost their lives or their loved ones in this forgotten case of ethnic cleansing. The "collective guilt" placed upon them because of their ancestors' country of origin cast a blanket of silence concerning their suffering. For most of the world this is a story that is difficult to believe. Others have said it was well deserved.

After the close of the Yugoslav prison camps in the fall of 1948, ethnic Germans who survived were forced to sign labor contracts that made them slaves in their own country. Many fled Yugoslavia, relocating in Austria, Germany, Canada, the United States, and other countries around the world. Today, the little German village of Glogon, Yugoslavia, has become Glogonj, Serbia, and the German families who managed to survive are spread across many nations.

We tell this story to honor the life of a little Yugoslav girl named Josie, and in memory of all people who have suffered and died during wartime atrocities. The true story of war is not told in the biographies of great wartime generals, presidents, or kings. It is revealed in the daily lives of powerless people who struggle to survive in war-torn lands. This book is based on the true story of Josie Trollmann, and we have made every attempt to recreate it as accurately as possible.

Susan Lowe, Josie's daughter, and Diane Iverson, Josie's niece

St. Anna's Catholic Church, Glogon, Yugoslavia

CHAPTER 1

Glogon, Yugoslavia, October 1944

• • •

"ANDREAS, WAIT FOR ME!" JOSIE gasped.

Whitewashed farmhouses faded into dense autumn fog, and bare mulberry trees stood like skeletons along the village streets as Josie ran through waist-high grass. Her sweater blew open, chilling her as she struggled to keep up with her lanky twelve-year-old brother. Damp, ripe grass stung as it slapped against her legs.

Whipping around, Andreas walked backward with his hands cupped around his mouth and barked toward his younger sister.

"You know the way, Josie. Take your doll and go home!"

Pumping her small legs faster, Josie worked even harder to catch up. She knew he didn't want her to tag along. She had heard him complain to *Oma* that none of the other boys in Glogon had to take their baby sisters everywhere. *Oma* said she didn't care if all the boys in Yugoslavia didn't have to take their baby sisters. *Opa* would take a switch to him if he left her crying one more time. After all, he was eight years older and should be glad to look after her.

Clenching her small mouth into a straight line, she continued pushing against the wind. "I'm almost five years old. I'm not a baby," thought Josie.

Andreas's wavy brown hair was blowing in the breeze. Pulling his coat tighter against his slender frame, he slowed his pace. He began dragging a stick through the grass, allowing Josie to catch up with him.

He grumbled, "Hurry up!" Tossing the stick away, he reached down for her hand.

Catching her breath, Josie firmly grasped her rag doll with the brown button eyes that looked like her own.

Still out of breath, she smiled up at her brother, searching his eyes to see if he was still annoyed with her. Tentatively she said, "Where are we going?"

He grumbled back, "I am going to play marbles with Karl. You are going to sit across the street and watch."

Turning away from the wind, Josie pushed her golden-brown hair out of her face and stammered, "But I want to play." Her brown eyes brimmed with tears.

Andreas suddenly tugged on her arm, pulling them both to a quick stop. Startled, Josie looked up into the angry face of a uniformed soldier towering in front of them. He wore a narrow cap with a red star on the front. Andreas gulped as the soldier placed his big gun over his shoulder;

she could feel her brother's hand tremble as his fingers tightened around her hand.

The soldier looked sternly into Andreas's eyes. "No *Kinder* on this street!" he ordered in broken German. "Return to your home at once!" Josie pressed closer to her brother.

"Yes sir," Andreas croaked as they both turned to run.

The afternoon was getting colder as they raced back across the field. Gripping Josie's hand, Andreas picked up speed. Her arm ached, but not wanting to be left behind she tried her best to keep up with him. They ran all the way to *Haupt Gasse*, the street where they lived, before daring to glance back. Realizing that the soldier was no longer in sight, Josie let a sigh escape from her lips as relief washed its way through her little body.

Andreas lessened his grip on Josie's hand and let it slip out of his as he slowed down. Panting, she said, "Andreas, are you going to tell *Mutter* and *Opa* that we saw a Russian soldier today?"

"No," he whispered. "Everybody already knows they're here. They took most of the town's horses, even *Opa*'s. Don't you say anything either," he warned. "We'll only get in trouble for crossing the field without permission."

Josie nodded. She had heard the grown-ups whispering about the Russian and Serbian soldiers just before she fell asleep last night. *Mutter* had told them that a soldier had stolen one of her friends gold teeth, right out of her mouth. Josie had wanted to ask how that was possible, but didn't want her mother and grandparents to know she had been listening.

Looking ahead, she could see the house where she and Andreas lived with *Mutter* and their father's parents, Trollmann *Oma* and *Opa*. Their home was almost hidden behind the white brick fence that enclosed their large yard. The thick window shutters and heavy whitewashed walls felt reassuring today.

Andreas began kicking a rock across the granite stone road when Josie tugged on his coat sleeve.

"What do you want now!" he snapped.

"Can you teach me to play marbles when we get home?" she asked.

"Don't be silly. Girls don't play marbles," he replied.

Josie's lip began to quiver as her eyes filled with tears for the second time today. Pushing her up the steps to the front door ahead of him, Andreas dropped his voice. "Let's make wagons with *Oma*'s sewing spools." They scraped their muddy shoes on the boot-scraper before opening the door.

The inviting fragrance of *Oma*'s dinner drifted out to meet them. Josie felt thankful to be home. She closed the heavy door securely and leaned against the hard wooden barrier between her family and the outside world. As she glanced around the room, her sense of safety quickly disappeared.

Trollmann *Oma* stood, hands on her hips, frowning at Josie and Andreas. With *Oma*'s braided gray hair twisted into a bun, and that mean look on her face, Josie thought she looked almost as frightening as the soldier they had seen earlier. "Where have you two been?" *Oma* asked without a hint of her usual smile.

Andreas avoided the question. "The goulash smells great, *Oma*. When do we eat?"

Pushing him back toward the door, Trollmann *Oma* barked, "You'll eat after your chores are done! The men have not returned from working on the airport. Go feed the cows and pigs before it turns dark." As Andreas headed toward the animal stalls, she added, "Don't forget to bring water from the well when you come back."

Oma wiped her flour-dusted hands across the front of her worn apron. Her face softened as she leaned down and placed a hand on either side of Josie's face. "Now, little one, tell me where the two of you have been."

Josie glanced toward the cattle stalls, not wanting to make Andreas mad.

"*Liebling*, what is it?" asked Trollmann *Oma*.

"I promised Andreas I would help," insisted Josie as she averted her eyes from her grandmother. Quickly tossing her doll aside she bolted back out the door. Andreas was her big brother, and she would be very careful to keep their secret.

CHAPTER 2

The Terrible Truth

• • •

PUZZLED, JOSIE LOOKED AT HER family gathered around the large wooden table in their kitchen. She smiled at her mother's parents, Wurtz *Opa* and Wurtz *Oma*. They lived nearby and were visiting for dinner. *Opa* looked as though he didn't feel well; his face was gray and puffy. Josie was amazed at how quiet everyone was. The only noise was Andreas swishing bread around his bowl to soak up all the Goulash broth. Usually, when the Wurtz grandparents visited, the women spoke of sewing projects or discussed how tomatoes or beans were coming along in the garden. Wurtz *Opa* and Trollmann *Opa* would be loudly discussing a problem concerning the cows or pigs. They might talk of a shelter they needed to build, crops to harvest, or a wheel that needed to be repaired on the old wagon. Suddenly she noticed that Trollmann *Opa* was missing.

"*Mutter*, where is Trollmann *Opa*? Isn't he hungry?" she asked, breaking the silence.

Mutter stared down at her plate but didn't answer. It was Wurtz *Oma* who spoke; her voice was hoarse. "Just eat your Goulash. Now is a time for eating, not asking questions."

Josie swallowed a few more bites, watching her mother and grandmothers exchange brief glances, tears welling up in their eyes. *Mutter* stood up quietly. Placing her arm around Trollmann *Oma*, she led her out of the room.

"*Mutter*, what's wrong?" Josie called after them.

Wurtz *Opa* reached across the table and squeezed Josie's arm. Whispering, he said, "They are sad that Trollmann *Opa* did not come home today."

Ignoring his food for the first time, Andreas let a crust of bread slip into his bowl. "Is something wrong with Trollmann *Opa*?"

Josie slid across the wooden bench to be closer to Andreas. She had an uneasy feeling in her stomach.

Wurtz *Opa*'s shoulders slumped forward as he pushed his plate away. Leaning back he began filling his pipe with tobacco. "I don't know, Andreas. I don't know." Tamping the tobacco deeper into the pipe, he said, more to himself than to anyone in the room, "We should have left with the German soldiers. These Russian and Serb soldiers are savages."

Andreas sat up straight and turned toward *Opa*. "But, *Opa*, I thought we didn't like the German soldiers when they were in Glogon."

"We didn't like how they treated the Serbs, but these Russian and Serb soldiers don't like us." *Opa* grimaced. Josie wondered if he was going to be sick. Turning his face away from the table he mumbled, "They think that we are Nazi sympathizers. We must be very careful not to make them angry."

Surprised, Andreas asked, "Why would they think that? What did we do?"

Running his fingers over his thick mustache, Wurtz *Opa* sighed. "They don't like us because we're German."

"Well, that's stupid!" Andreas exclaimed. "*Opa*, we were born German. It's not something we did."

"That is not the way they see it, Andreas," said Wurtz *Opa*. Getting up, he walked across the room to turn up the wick on the dimming kerosene lamp.

Wurtz *Oma* lowered her voice as she leaned across the table. "Children, remember this," she said. "You must never judge a person by where they or their ancestors were born, but by how that person treats you. Do not be angry with all of the soldiers."

"That's enough!" Wurtz *Opa* ordered from the other side of the room. "You are talking too much. Andreas, dinner is over. Go and help Josie get ready for bed."

Confused, Josie noticed again that her strong grandfather did not look so strong tonight. Carefully watching his tired eyes, she walked toward Wurtz *Opa*. Placing her hand on his worn sleeve, she asked hesitantly, "When is Trollmann *Opa* coming home?"

"I said it is time for bed, little one. Go and dream about your doll." Wurtz *Opa* patted her on the head, but he sounded far away.

Andreas grabbed Josie's hand and pulled her toward their bedroom. Once through the doorway, he stopped suddenly, causing Josie to run into him. Andreas pulled Josie in front of him as he backed up slowly. Standing still, they could hear Wurtz *Oma* raise her voice. "Why did you tell her to dream of her doll when her Trollmann *Opa* is not coming home? Why didn't you tell them? It will not be easier in the morning."

Trying to break free, Josie could feel Andreas's arm tighten against her as his hand clamped across her mouth. "Shh," he whispered as they stood against the wall listening.

Andreas and Josie could hear Wurtz *Opa* knocking his pipe against the top of the farm table. *Opa*'s voice sounded hard and cold. "Should I tell them that their *Vater* was forced to join the German army or be killed? Should I tell them he may be dead anyway?"

Josie glanced into Andreas's eyes in the dimly lit room. She knew, even though his hand had dropped from her mouth, that he wanted her to remain quiet. She stood frozen as they continued to lean against the cool wall, listening.

Wurtz *Opa* was still talking. "Should I tell them that those Serbian soldiers you want them not to judge lied about having us work on an airport for the town? Should I tell them the men of this town have been going out to work every day, only to find out that we were digging our own graves? Should I tell them that most of Glogon's German men were shot today, that their Trollmann *Opa* lies dead in the trench he helped to dig..." His voice broke, but he soon continued more softly, "that I should be dead also? You tell me, Anna, is that what I should tell them? Even Father Knapp is dead. Andreas is one of his altar boys. How are we going to tell him that he doesn't need to report to the church tomorrow morning because our priest was murdered?" *Opa* seemed to choke before continuing. "Now, why would they kill a priest?"

Wurtz *Oma* began crying, "It is not your fault that the Serbian soldier recognized you. It was God's blessing that today you were wearing that old work hat your Serb friend gave you. This allowed that good soldier to pull you away from certain death, and for that I am grateful."

Andreas and Josie sat together in silence. She pushed closer to her brother, burying her face against his chest as he wrapped his arms around her. His tears fell against her hair, and she sobbed quietly as they began rocking back and forth. She struggled to understand what she had just heard. *Could Trollmann* Opa *really be dead? Did that mean he was never coming back? And what did Wurtz* Opa *mean about her dad?*

CHAPTER 3

Soldiers at the Door

• • •

Josie lay in bed watching the morning light filter through the bedroom window and listening to the hushed voices of *Mutter* and Trollmann *Oma* coming faintly through the bedroom window. They were in the backyard, where they were already busy with morning chores. She hoped they would be less sad than last night. *Mutter* and *Oma* had both been crying a lot lately. Maybe she could cheer them up with a bouquet of flowers. As she pulled the pink and green quilt up around her, she remembered that it had snowed just a few days ago. There would be no flowers left in *Oma*'s garden.

The rooster crowed enthusiastically somewhere in the yard beyond *Mutter* and *Oma*. Josie knew they were feeding chickens behind the house, and she was sure they had gathered fresh eggs for breakfast. Thinking about it made her hungry. She pulled her rag doll back from the edge of the bed and snuggled into the warmth of her quilts. Soon *Oma* was clanking heavy pans on the wood cook stove in the kitchen. Josie knew Andreas was still sleeping soundly because she could hear his gentle snoring from under the cocoon of quilts across the room. She thought about what she would like to eat with her eggs. She could smell warm homemade bread and she pictured *Mutter*'s apricot jam. Her stomach growled at the thought. Hmm.

There was a sudden, harsh pounding on the front door. Frightened, Josie sat up in bed.

She pulled the quilt tighter and looked over at Andreas. He sat wide-eyed in his bed, startled from his dreams. His bare feet dropped quickly to the braided wool rug between their beds as he tossed the quilts back. The pounding became more insistent.

Josie almost ran into Andreas as they both raced toward the doorway. Tumbling into the hall, they froze. Trollmann *Oma* rushed to unbolt the front door; as she pulled it open, two Serbian soldiers stood on either side of the door with their guns drawn and aimed at *Oma* and *Mutter*. Josie's stomach did flips, and she was afraid that she would get sick.

"Everybody out!" ordered one of the soldiers.

Josie and Andreas stood unmoving as *Mutter* and Trollmann *Oma* pleaded for time for the children to dress before leaving the house. Josie gasped as one of the soldiers stomped toward them and grabbed Andreas roughly by his nightshirt.

"How old are you?" the soldier demanded.

Josie trembled as Andreas fought to find his voice.

"Leave him be. You can see he is only a child," said the second soldier, who then pushed Andreas back toward Josie and *Mutter.* "Hurry up! Get dressed! Now!"

"*Mutter...?*" Josie whispered uncertainly.

Leaning gently toward her, *Mutter* whispered back, "Dress quickly and pray for God to protect us."

Josie and Andreas hurried back to their room. Josie pulled a dress on over her nightclothes and struggled to put on socks and shoes. Andreas buttoned his wool vest then quickly laced his boots. He grabbed Josie's arm and pulled her back toward the hall just as she pressed her foot into her second shoe.

Moments later, Josie was pushed past two more soldiers. These men were lying on their stomachs on either side of the steps with machine guns aimed at her family. *What's going on? Why are they mad at us,* Josie wondered.

She stumbled over her untied shoelace, and *Mutter* quickly reached to catch her. With a harsh blow from the butt of his rifle, a soldier struck *Mutter* in the shoulder, forcing her toward the front gate and into the street. Josie had to hurry to keep up.

She looked around at the growing crowd of neighbors. "Where are all the men?" she asked.

"There may not be any men left in Glogon," *Mutter* whispered in a strange voice.

With surprise, Josie noticed that many of their neighbors were also being forced from their homes and pushed into the middle of the cobblestone street. Everyone seemed as confused and afraid as she was. Children and mothers were weeping as they held on to one another.

Looking around, she could see Trollmann *Oma* ahead of them in the crowd. She called Trollmann *Oma*'s name, but her grandmother didn't turn around. Josie tried again to raise her voice over the cries of the women and children around her. Still she got no response. Wiping tears from her cheeks, she strained to see past the adults towering in front of her. She was afraid that if she lost sight of Trollmann *Oma* she would never see her again.

Josie knew she should be glad that Wurtz *Oma* and Wurtz *Opa* had not stayed over last night, but she wished *Opa* were here to keep them safe. Hopping up and down, she searched the crowd for *Opa*. Only a few of the town's men were walking in the group. She couldn't see *Opa* anywhere.

"Josie," *Mutter* grabbed her arm and whispered sternly. "You must walk quietly. We don't want to draw the soldiers' attention to us. Andreas, hold your sister's other hand."

Josie continued to walk slowly, lowering her face as tears streamed down her already wet cheeks. When they reached the edge of Glogon, she could see a big barbed wire fence that surrounded several old houses in front of them. Many of their friends and neighbors were already trapped behind the fence.

"How will Wurtz *Opa* and *Oma* know where we have gone?" she asked. "Will they be able to get through the fence to find us?"

CHAPTER 4

The Cellar

• • •

Josie bit her lower lip as she looked around the fenced-in area that some of the adults were calling the holding camp. Barbed wire enclosed a dozen houses at the edge of Glogon. Guards walked silently around the edges of the fence with guns on their shoulders. She turned to Andreas, pulling on his sleeve to get his attention.

"Andreas, when will *Mutter* and *Oma* be back?"

She could feel his arm trembling as he put it around her.

"Don't worry. They will be back. Besides, I'm here."

The day dragged on as old women and children from town were forced into the already crowded area. For most people, there had been nothing to eat since dinner at home the night before. The adults talked urgently about hungry children or discussed farm animals that needed to be milked and fed; most seemed to be talking to themselves. Some of them were wringing their hands as they paced around in meaningless circles. The frightened looks in their eyes made Josie's stomach ache. Hungry dogs could be heard barking from distant yards, but nothing could be done.

Several children had gathered together. Josie watched as the older boys took turns trying to balance sticks on the backs of their hands. She almost laughed as Andreas, having lasted longer than the others, raised his hand in victory.

The laughter stuck in her throat as she remembered *Mutter* and *Oma* hadn't been allowed into this area at the same time as she and Andreas; stretching up on her tippy toes, Josie searched desperately to find them in the latest group of women to arrive. Although she was not able to see either of them, she noticed a neighbor woman leaning against one of the buildings. She started to tell Andreas where she was going, but at the last minute decided not to break his concentration during this next round. Slipping away from the group, Josie ran to the woman.

"Have you seen my *Mutter* or Trollmann *Oma?*"

Kneeling beside her, the woman picked a piece of straw out of Josie's uncombed hair and held her close.

"*Frau*, have you seen my *Mutter* or Trollmann *Oma?*" She asked again.

"They are locked in the cellar with several other women." The woman pointed toward the far house, across the enclosure. "Your Wurtz *Oma* is also in that dark hole. Go quietly and cry for the soldier to let your Wurtz *Oma* out. Keep crying until they release her."

As Josie started back to tell Andreas, the woman grabbed her shoulder.

"Go now," she insisted. "There isn't much time!"

Ignoring the feeling in the pit of her stomach, Josie ran toward the house as fast as her legs would carry her. Reaching its cellar, she dropped to her knees and began pounding her little fists with all her might. Splinters worked their way into the soft flesh of her hands as she continued to pummel against the slanted wooden door of the underground storage room that held her *Mutter* and two grandmothers as prisoners.

"Wurtz *Oma*! Wurtz *Oma*!"

The guard jerked Josie away from the door. "Stop that at once!"

Ignoring him she continued kicking and screaming, "*Oma*! I need my Wurtz *Oma*! Please, let my *Oma* out!"

Lifting her up until her dusty shoes no longer touched the ground, the guard swung her through the air and then dumped her roughly at the feet of the women who had gathered around.

"Keep this brat away from me!" The guard shouted.

Avoiding the attempts of the women to restrain her, Josie picked herself up and stumbled back to the cellar door. Flinging herself on the edge of the step, she glared at the soldier who was now ignoring her. Laying her swollen face in her hands, she begged.

"Please let my Wurtz *Oma* out."

Taking his gun off of his shoulder, the frustrated soldier pulled Josie away and threw open the heavy cellar door.

"What is your *Oma*'s name?"

Josie looked up at the soldier. "Wurtz *Oma*," she answered.

The guard disappeared into the darkness of the cellar where Josie could hear women crying and calling out.

Later as Josie sat beside one of the fenced houses, curled in Wurtz *Oma*'s lap, she felt a lump like a stone in her throat. *Oma* whispered soothingly and gently as she rubbed Josie's back, but nothing helped. *Mutter* and Trollmann *Oma* were still locked in the cold, dark cellar. Why hadn't she asked for them? Why didn't she ask for her *Mutter*? Lying on Wurtz *Oma*'s lap, she felt a heavy sadness settle deep into her bones. She prayed that her mother and Trollmann *Oma* would forgive her.

CHAPTER 5

Alone in Franzfeld, Late 1945

• • •

JOSIE PUSHED THE ITCHY STRAW away from her face and sat up on the cold hardwood floor. Shivering, she looked around for Andreas. She had slept in her coat, but she was still cold. Seeing Andreas on the floor next to her, she leaned quietly toward him. Several others in the crowded room were beginning to stir, but many still slept.

"Andreas," she whispered.

Josie laughed softly as she watched him attempt to brush the straw away from his face.

"What!" he snapped, sounding annoyed. A baby in the next room started to cry.

Fighting a smile, she said, "I'm sorry I laughed. The straw in your hair looks funny."

"What do you want?" he asked, still sounding cross.

"I'm hungry," Josie said, lowering her eyes. She hadn't meant to make her brother angry. Since they had been moved to Franzfeld, Yugoslavia, he was the only family she had left. They were many miles from home, and they had no idea where *Mutter* and their grandparents were.

Andreas sat up and pulled straw from his hair with his fingers. "I know, me too. The guards will bring the soup soon."

Josie couldn't stop shaking. "I want to go home."

An old woman from across the room came over to Josie. Turning her around, she placed a hand on each shoulder and said, *"Kinder,* you are not going to go home. None of us are ever going home. You must stop thinking about such things."

"That's not true!" Josie gasped as she pulled away and ran out of the room. Hearing Andreas call to her as the front door slammed shut, she plopped down on the top step and waited for him to catch up. A moment later the door flew back open and he sat down beside her.

"Josie! Don't run away when I am calling you. It is not safe."

Wiping tears from her sunken cheeks, she swallowed hard. "I want to go home. I want to see *Mutter* and *Oma.* I want to sleep in my bed. I hate it here."

Andreas picked a piece of straw from her hair and threw it on the dirt in the yard. Quietly he said, "We all want to go home, but nobody is there. *Mutter* is at a work camp. She is not at home. Josie, I heard some of the older women talking last night after you fell asleep. They think that Wurtz *Oma* and Wurtz *Opa* are still in Glogon working for a family of Serbs."

"Then let's go to *Oma*'s," she suggested.

Choking up, he continued, "We can't go there either. Someone thought they were being forced to sleep in the cattle stalls! The Serb family is living in their house."

Josie gritted her teeth and spit her words out one at a time: "I hate this place!"

Placing his arm around her thin shoulders, Andreas held her as she cried.

After what seemed like a long time, he said, "Josie, remember that *Mutter* and *Oma* wanted us to pray for our safety every morning and every night. Well, we haven't prayed this morning."

Taking a deep breath, Josie turned around and knelt on the bottom step. She watched Andreas fold his hands on his lap and bow his head. Bowing her head also, she began, "Father in Heaven, please keep my family safe and let us all be together soon. And, if it's not too much trouble, could we all have sausage, eggs, and strudel today? Oh, and God, I would like milk, too."

Startled, Josie felt herself being yanked to her feet by a passing soldier. He growled at her, "Tell the others to get their bowls. The food line is open."

Her stomach rumbling, Josie almost knocked Andreas over as she raced to open the door. She grabbed the doorknob, then paused and looked back at her brother. Giving him a small smile, she bowed her head again. "And, God, please make the soldiers nicer."

Throwing the door open, she yelled at the top of her lungs, "Breakfast!"

She ran to find her bowl in the corner and then hurried to catch up with Andreas. Her nose told her there would not be sausage and eggs, but she was thankful for anything that pushed back the hunger for a little while.

CHAPTER 6

Escape by Night

● ● ●

JOSIE SAT IN THE DIRT, leaning her back against the small house she and Andreas shared with thirty other people. She pulled her knees up to her chest, wrapped her arms around them, and tried not to shiver. Her coat no longer fit her. She could see her breath in the cold air, but she didn't want to go into the house until it was absolutely necessary. Inside, the straw was infested with bugs. The washtub had been taken out of the house with the rest of the furniture. Everyone took sponge baths with water from the well, but there was no soap and it was impossible to stay clean. Josie missed getting into the tub of warm water *Mutter* used to pour for her. She even missed the lye soap her grandmothers used to make. How long had it been since she had taken a bath? She couldn't remember.

Scooting over, she tried to catch part of the fading sun, hoping to warm up. She watched the boys tossing sticks back and forth next to the barbed wire fence. Out of the corner of her eye she could see the guards walking along the fence line with guns thrown over their shoulders. She stiffened as one of the guards stopped and yelled at the boys, "Get away from the fence!"

"Why are most of the guards so mean?" she whispered to herself. Seeing her brother running in her direction she jumped up and dusted the dirt off of her worn dress.

Andreas scolded, "Josie, what are you doing outside? It's almost dark."

"I didn't want to go in until I had to," she said, trembling more from anxiety than cold. Andreas nodded in understanding. "I was afraid the guard who yelled at you was going to take you away," she whimpered, shaking. "I'll die if something happens to you."

"Don't worry about him. He just warned us to get away from the fence. I'm not going anywhere."

"But, they took us away from *Mutter* and our *Omas* and *Opas*. What will I do if they take you away, Andreas?"

He hugged her tightly and dropped his voice to a whisper. "I have a plan. I saw a part of the fence where the wire doesn't touch the ground. I think we could crawl under it."

Josie's stared up at her older brother. "Where would we go?"

Andreas was quiet for a moment. "I overheard one of the new people the guards brought to the camp telling someone that *Mutter*, and Wurtz *Oma*, and *Opa* are still back in Glogon. I think they have been moved to another farm."

Josie wiped her sleeve across her eyes. Her lips trembling, she asked, "Why haven't they come to get us?"

Sounding impatient, Andreas clenched his teeth. "They can't. They are being guarded. They still have to work in the fields to help the Serbs farm the land." Raising his voice just a little he added, "Someone said they are giving all of Glogon's houses to the Serbs."

"But what if they catch us?"

"Josie, we are hungry every day. How many days can we eat dried bread and watered down soup?" Dust formed as he stomped his foot. "The old women are even putting weeds in the soup so we will feel less hungry." More softly, he added, "And you cry yourself to sleep every night. What could be worse?"

"What if we can't find Glogon?" she asked. "It took a long time to get here when we left the holding camp."

Andreas sighed. "I know the way. I was on the road once with *Opa*. Franzfeld is not that far from Glogon. I can find our way back home. I know I can."

"Maybe we should talk to the others about leaving?" Sniffling, she added, "We could all go."

Andreas narrowed his eyes and hissed at her in a voice so low she almost couldn't hear him. "No! We can't tell anyone. Don't you understand?" His voice sounded hoarse.

"They won't miss two kids, Josie, but they would miss a whole house of people. We need to go alone. Tonight, after everyone's asleep."

Nodding, Josie placed her small hand in her brother's larger one and let him lead her inside the house. Finding their corner, she lay down quietly and covered herself with her small coat, trying to keep warm. Her heart was beating hard against her chest as she thought about what Andreas had said. Closing her eyes, she prayed that God would help them find *Mutter*.

Later that night, while everyone else slept, Josie scooted quickly under the wire fence as her brother pulled the bottom wire as high as he could. Her heart was pounding when it was her turn to hold the lowest wire high enough for Andreas to slip under. She tugged and tugged, but couldn't pull it up any further.

"A little higher," he said, trying to squeeze under it.

"I can't do it. The guard is going to come back any time," she whispered frantically.

"Go and hide behind the shrubs." Andreas pointed behind her. "I'll be right there."

"I can't leave you," she pleaded. Again, she clenched the wire with both of her hands and felt it cut into her tender flesh as she struggled to lift it.

"Go!" he ordered.

She thought she could make out the shape of the guard in the distance. "Andreas, he's coming. Move out of the way and let me come back to your side," she pleaded.

"No. Go now!"

"But Andreas…" she started. Her heart was thumping in her chest.

"Go!" he repeated.

He had been so loud Josie was sure the guard had heard him. Her stomach turned and she thought she might throw up. Her legs felt like mush, but she forced herself away from the fence toward the shrubs.

Once she was behind the branches she could see Andreas digging with his hands in the dirt. A moment later he had rolled to her side of the fence and was quickly filling in the hole. Letting her breath out, she stood up, hoping he could see her in the darkness. Andreas flattened to the ground as the guard passed between two buildings and disappeared again. Rising to his feet, he moved quietly toward her. Josie glanced up at the starless sky and was thankful for the cloud cover. "Thank you, God," she whispered.

CHAPTER 7

The Dangerous Journey

• • •

JOSIE'S LEGS ACHED FROM WALKING. "I can't keep going, Andreas," she said. "I'm tired."

"We need to keep going," Andreas insisted. "We want to be a long way from Franzfeld before anyone notices we're gone."

Stopping defiantly, she dropped to the ground and began to cry. "I c-can't. I'm cold." Her teeth chattered as she spoke. Andreas pulled her back to her feet. "P-p-please, Andreas," she whined.

"Look," he said, pointing. "There's a cornfield just ahead of us. We can walk through it, and we'll be protected from the wind. No one will see us when the sun comes up. Come on, I'll race you."

Josie let him pull her forward, but it was too hard to run. Her legs felt numb and her face hurt from the cold.

It seemed to take forever to reach the field. Once there, Andreas insisted they walk deep into the tall stalks so they wouldn't be seen from the road. Finally, he stopped and sat down abruptly, making a crackling sound against the dry leaves. He was satisfied with the distance they had put between themselves and Franzfeld.

Josie stumbled into his back, almost falling. "That hurts!" she screamed into the darkness.

"Watch where you're going, and don't yell," he snapped back.

Josie was so angry that she thought of kicking him, but she was too exhausted. Falling down onto the dirt next to him, she asked, "Where are we?"

"We're on our way home," Andreas assured her. "I think we can be there tomorrow."

"It's so cold. Where are we going to sleep tonight?" she asked.

"Right here," he said, patting the ground. "The corn stalks will block most of the wind. Let's rest and we'll find *Mutter* tomorrow."

Josie scooted closer to her brother, and the two of them curled up at the base of the dry stalks with their arms wrapped tightly around each other. Shivering, she listened to the cold wind whipping through the tops of the cornstalks and wished for the warm blankets from her bed at home. She prayed that Andreas would be right and they would find their family in the morning. Pulling her arms up into the sleeves of her thin, tattered dress she pressed closer to her brother for warmth. Tears froze on her cheeks. She was surprised to find that she missed the warmth of the dirty straw on the floor of the house where they slept in Franzfeld.

The next morning Josie awakened to find a blanket of snow. In spite of the overhanging shelter of corn leaves, she and Andreas had been dusted with snow as they slept. Sitting up, she nudged Andreas until he was also awake. She watched him blink in amazement as he looked around. She brushed the snow out of her hair and stood up. Her legs and back were stiff, but she felt better than she had last night. She wiggled her icy fingers to warm them. The sun was up and although the air was cold, it was warmer than the night before. The world beyond the cornfield was sparkling white. She scooped up a handful of snow and threw it at Andreas.

"Hey!" he shouted as it hit him in the face. He made his own snowball and tossed it in her direction.

"You missed!" she giggled. Knowing that he probably wouldn't miss again, she began running as quickly as she could through the tall stalks. Looking over her shoulder, she saw Andreas getting closer. He threw a snowball that hit her in the back. She pushed her legs harder as she pressed through the field and onto the open road.

"Whoa!" commanded a man to his team of horses. He was driving a large old farm sleigh toward her.

Josie screeched to a stop and stared at the two men sitting in the sleigh. She took an uneasy step back toward the cornfield when she saw their hats and realized they were Serbian. A moment later, Andreas jumped out of the field and tugged Josie back to the edge of the road.

"Sorry," he panted. Watching the men, he dropped his snowball.

The men mumbled something to each other. The driver then yelled, "Giddy up!" as the horses began to pull the sleigh down the road. Josie and Andreas stood still, watching the sleigh grow smaller in the distance.

"That was close," Andreas whispered. Josie nodded.

Unable to speak, she remembered *Mutter's* reminder to pray for safety. *Dear God*, she thought, *please help us get home safely.*

"Josie," Andreas said, shaking her arm, "Why are you just standing there?"

"I was praying," she said, finding her voice.

"Well, you had better start walking if you want to find *Mutter* today," he said impatiently. "Come on, let's follow this road. I think it will take us to Glogon. We'll walk near the cornfield. If we hear anyone coming we'll hide in the corn."

They hadn't walked far when Josie pointed, "Look Andreas, it's the Serbs again. They are waiting by their sleigh. What if they want to take us back to the camp?"

"Run!" Andreas screamed as he pushed Josie back into the cornfield. Andreas followed closely behind her, and her hair whipped against his face as they ran.

"Wait!" one of the men shouted in broken German. "We won't hurt you. We want to help."

Josie tripped and fell in the snow. Andreas helped her to her feet. She attempted to run again, but she slipped back to her knees. The driver of the sleigh quickly caught up to them. Andreas shoved Josie behind him.

"It's OK," the man said. "I want to help. Let us give you a ride. You are a long way from a town."

Stepping from behind Andreas, Josie smiled. "I think God sent you."

"Maybe so, little one." Looking at Andreas he asked, "Where are you headed?"

"To Glogon." Andreas hesitated, "We're going to our family."

The man nodded. He seemed to understand. "My friend and I are going through Glogon. We'll let you out at the edge of town."

Andreas reached out his hand, "Thank you, I'm An..."

"No names!" interrupted the man. Less sternly he added, "It's a dangerous time. It's better if we do not exchange names."

"Are you Serbs?" asked Josie.

"Yes, little one. Not all Serbs hate Germans."

"Oh, I know. That's what my *Oma* told me." Josie's stomach growled noisily.

"You have a smart *Oma*," laughed the man. "Let's get back to the sleigh and feed that stomach of yours."

Josie and Andreas crawled into the back of the farm sleigh under a tent of blankets. They sat on a sheepskin coat that belonged to one of the men. Both of them devoured the bread and sausage the men shared with them. As the sleigh slid over the fresh snow, Josie stuck her head out from under the warm blankets and called out over the noise of sleigh and horses, "Yum, this is the best sausage I have ever eaten!"

"Quiet," warned the driver. "I'm glad you like it, but there must be no more talking. If someone hears you, we will all have trouble. When it is time to stop, do not speak until one of us tells you it is safe to come out."

"Are you taking us to our house?" asked Josie.

"Don't be stupid," laughed Andreas. "They don't know where we live."

"We'll stop near the edge of town," said the driver, interrupting their banter. "It will be dark by then and you can find your way through town unnoticed." With sorrow in his voice he added, "Your family is probably not living in your old house. You will need to ask if anyone knows them, but be careful."

With the softness of the sheepskin against their faces, the warmth of the blankets and the gliding rhythm of the heavy sleigh, it wasn't long before both Josie and Andreas found it hard to keep their eyes open. They slept soundly and awakened only when the cold air hit their faces as one of the men pulled the blankets back.

"It's time to go," the driver whispered, lifting Josie from the back of the sleigh bed. Jumping down, Andreas grabbed Josie's hand, pulling her into the darkness.

"Thank you," he called back to the men, "God bless you!"

"Go with God," the men replied in unison, and the sleigh turned onto the snow-covered cobblestone road of Glogon's main street.

CHAPTER 8

Searching for Family

• • •

"ANDREAS, LOOK!" JOSIE POINTED TOWARD St. Anna's Catholic Church in Glogon. It was the first time in a long time that she felt like she knew where she was. Staring upward she took in the sight of the steeple against the darkening sky. She wanted to run into the church and sit in the carved wooden pew where her family often sat. She pictured the women with black scarves covering their heads and beautiful dresses with fancy shawls around their shoulders. She could almost hear the sound of the church bell that caused everyone to beam when it clanged on Sunday mornings. Squinting, she was able to see the brick columns and the iron gate of the cemetery that surrounded the beautiful building. Breathing in deeply, she could almost smell the incense, see the lights of the chandelier hanging over the church alter and feel the excitement of a Christmas Eve Midnight Mass. She wondered how many

Christmas celebrations they had missed. She pictured Wurtz *Opa* and Trollmann *Opa* playing cards on the wooden table in the kitchen, while *Mutter* and the *Omas* visited as they baked strudel and made Christmas cookies. Thinking of it made her mouth water. She thought of *Vater* breaking a cookie as he winked at *Mutter*, but she couldn't remember his face anymore. She did remember that she and Andreas would stare at the glowing candles and colorful candies that hung on the tree. It seemed like such a long time ago. Her throat ached as the sweetness of past experiences rushed over her.

"Josie," whispered Andreas, startling her away from her memories. "Come on! It isn't safe to stay out in the open. We need to find someone we know who can tell us where to find *Mutter*." She didn't need any more coaxing as the church's door flew open and a laughing soldier shoved a woman in a torn dress out the door. Josie felt her earlier meal working its way back into her throat as he continued to mock the woman and yell bad words at her as she lay crumpled in the street.

Quietly Andreas took her hand and pulled her further back into the shadows; the two of them slowly crept through the thickening darkness. They stopped at each house to listen for familiar voices. In the night the white-washed houses with dark tiled roofs all seemed alike.

"Andreas, do you think we could just go to the next house and ask if they know where *Mutter* might be?" Josie rubbed her arms frantically as her body shook from the cold damp air.

"That is a dumb idea," he answered. "If it turns out to be a house full of people who hate Germans, they might turn us in or even kill us!" Andreas shuddered. "Just keep listening for voices as we walk by the houses. Don't worry. We are going to find someone we know soon."

Josie hoped so; even with the thick blanket the men had given them wrapped around her thin shoulders, the tears that were forming in her eyes felt like they were freezing. It wasn't long before they thought they heard Wurtz *Oma*'s voice. Josie followed Andreas as they slipped through the shadowy remains of a garden toward the animal stalls connected to the back of the house.

"Don't make a sound," Andreas whispered. "Maybe we will hear her again and it will be safe to go in." They had been waiting in the cold night air for a long time, and Josie's freezing fingers hurt. Suddenly, they were startled when someone stepped out of the shadows.

"*Oma!*" Andreas threw his arms around her. "*Oma*, you're here!"

Wurtz *Oma* pulled both of them tightly to her breast. Josie squeezed her eyes shut, terrified that when she opened them she would wake up on the filthy straw-covered floor of their room at Franzfeld, and all of this would have been a dream. "*Oma*, I can't believe we found you," she said, nuzzling her icy face into the folds of her grandmother's apron.

"Josie! Andreas!" said *Oma*, her voice breaking with emotion. "Hurry! We must get you inside before you are seen!" Pulling them out of the night air and into the animal stalls behind the house, her arms trembled as she wrapped them around both of the *Kinder*. They clung to one another without saying a word for what seemed like a long time. "Thank God! Thank God!" *Oma* finally said.

Josie looked up into Wurtz *Oma*'s face, finally believing she and Andreas were safe with their family. Looking around she asked, "Why are we outside with the cows? Let's go inside and tell *Opa* we are here." In her excitement she rambled on, "Are *Mutter* and Trollmann *Oma* here too? They will be so surprised to see us!"

Wurtz *Oma* took both Josie and Andreas over to a wooden crate in the corner and sat them down. Kneeling down on the dirty straw in front of them, she whispered, "*Kinder, Opa* and your *Mutter* are still working in the fields this evening. They will be home soon. Trollmann *Oma* is working in a vineyard not far from here. She lives in a small shack with several other women. We will not see her tonight." Sweeping her arms out and motioning around her, *Oma* added, "This is our home for now."

"Why are you living outside like cattle?" Andreas demanded angrily.

"Shhhh," *Oma* dropped her voice. Looking around anxiously, she pulled both children close again. "Listen to me. Home is where your family is, and this is where we are today. Serb families have been given all of the houses in town. The government now says that the German people are not allowed to own property or belongings. They are letting those of us who are able to work tend a farm or work as house servants. For this we are allowed to live. We are fortunate to have this shelter to sleep in. Many people have nothing to keep them warm."

Andreas stood up and clenched both fists. His jaw tightened with anger. It frightened Josie. She was afraid he would start shouting. The people in the house might send for the guards to come and take them back to Franzfeld. She never wanted to go back there again.

"I hate the Serbs," hissed Andreas through his teeth.

Oma pulled him close to her. "Andreas, how can you hate them for being Serbs and say you don't understand why they hate us for being Germans? All Germans did not believe as Hitler did, and all Serbs do not believe as Tito does. This family provides us with food for the work we do and does not abuse us."

"How can you say that, *Oma?*" insisted Andreas. "You are living in an animal stall."

Standing up tall, Wurtz *Oma* straightened her apron. "That is enough. The two of you need to stay in the shadows. If someone comes, you must hide in the pile of straw in the back and be silent." Holding her chin up, she said, "I am going inside to cook the evening meal for the family that now lives in this house. When I am through, you will see that they will be good enough to give me a sufficient amount of food to feed our family. For this I thank them and God."

"Can I come with you?" asked Josie. She didn't want to wait in the shadows for *Opa* and *Mutter* to come home.

"Josie, it is against the law for you to be here. You must stay hidden." Sighing, she turned to Andreas and added, "There are some warm quilts on the wooden shelf behind you. Pull a couple down so that you will both stay warm while you wait to surprise your *Mutter*. She will be so relieved to see the two of you."

Both Josie and Andreas went silently to the haystack and lay down as *Oma* turned to go into the house. Andreas folded one quilt several times to make a pillow for the two of them and covered them both with the other. Neither of them had said a word since *Oma* went inside to care for the Serbian family's needs. Josie felt sick to her stomach. She hoped *Opa* and *Mutter* would be home soon.

Oma had been gone for quite a while. Josie and Andreas were drifting off to sleep when they were both startled by the rusty creaking of the stall door. Panic filled them as they quickly shifted into the darkness of the corner, ducking under the wooden shelf.

"I am so tired," *Mutter* sighed as she rubbed her neck with one hand.

"I will bring water. You need to wash those blisters," *Opa* told her.

"*Mutter*! *Opa*!" Andreas and Josie said at the same time.

Mutter dropped to her knees, sobbing, as she folded them into her arms. "My children! My children!" She kept repeating the words. *Opa* put his arms around all three of them, and that is the way *Oma* found them when she finally returned from her duties.

CHAPTER 9

Hiding

• • •

MUTTER GAVE ANDREAS AND JOSIE kisses and hugs before going out to the fields with *Opa*. They had been back with their family for a couple of weeks. "Remember to braid your hair, Josie. You don't want it to get tangled." She smiled and blew them another kiss before turning away. Josie remembered all too well the pain of having Wurtz *Oma* and *Mutter* comb the tangles from her matted hair.

The night they returned, *Mutter* and *Oma* cried when they saw the lice and fleabites that covered the children. *Opa* had insisted they wash themselves in the tub of water he brought in from the well. The bites hadn't bothered Josie nearly as much as having the tangles yanked out of her hair. It was hard to be quiet during the process, but she understood how dangerous any noise would be. She had gone from stifling tears to stifling giggles when she saw

Andreas in the large pair of men's trousers. *Opa* gave them to him because his old pair was falling apart. He looked so funny. He had no suspenders, so his pants were gathered around his middle with a piece of rope. Remembering made her smile.

Standing up and stretching, Josie ran her hands down the blue print dress that *Mutter* and *Oma* had made for her. It was altered from an old one that *Mutter* brought home when returning from the fields one day. *Mutter* took material from the bottom of the old dress and covered up the small hole in the bodice by making a pocket. Josie hadn't had a new dress in such a long time it was nice to have something clean to wear.

Pointing at her beautiful new pocket, she turned to Andreas and said, "Look." Grinning, she stuck her foot out so that he could also see the black shoes that *Opa* had found for her. Beaming she said, "*Opa* put rolled corn husks in the toes so the shoes would fit."

Rolling his eyes, Andreas snapped, "Who cares if you have new shoes and a new dress? If you keep eating like you have been, you will be too fat for the dress."

Josie glared at her older brother. "That is not true. You take it back!" she demanded, stomping her feet. "Besides, you're the one who ate two potatoes last night. Everyone else only got one." Plopping down on the hay she suddenly felt sad and confused. *Opa* kept worrying about her being too skinny and now her brother was calling her fat!

Andreas sat staring at her for a few moments. "Josie, I was just teasing," he mumbled. "Guess it wasn't funny."

She watched him roll over and run his hands over the floor behind him, searching for something. She wondered what he was looking for. His eyes darted toward the door that led to the house. They both knew they might have to bury themselves in the hay at any moment. Smiling, she saw his fingers brush the face of her new cornhusk doll. *Oma* had sewn on two tiny brown buttons for eyes that she said were just like Josie's. The doll was supposed to be for the last Christmas they had missed together. It felt good to hold a doll again.

"Hey! Look what I found," Andreas said, tossing the doll in Josie's direction. Reaching in the pocket of his baggy pants, he pulled out the corncob pipe that *Opa* had given him and ran his fingers over it. *Opa* had said when times were better Andreas might even get to smoke it.

Josie picked up her doll. Not wanting to stay angry with her brother, she pulled the worn quilt over her legs and scooted closer to him. The smoke from the chimney smelled so good. It was hard to understand why they couldn't go inside to warm themselves. If the family who now owned the house was being so nice to them like *Oma* kept saying, why weren't they willing to share the warmth of their wood stove? It just didn't seem Christian.

Noticing something move out of the corner of her eye, she leaned forward and peeked through the wooden slats of the wall and strained to see through the fading light. She could just make out the shape of a woman bending over. She hoped *Oma* would bring extra potatoes for tonight's meal. Her stomach was empty. "Is that *Oma* working in the garden?" she whispered.

"Yeah," Andreas answered. "I hope she was able to gather some eggs to go with the vegetables tonight."

"Me, too." Josie's stomach growled. She was happy to eat most anything besides wormy soup. Wanting to think about something else, she poked her brother in the side. "Andreas, will you tell me the story about Hansel and Gretel?"

"Aren't you tired of hearing the same story over and over?" he asked.

"I love to hear it, and you tell it a little different each time." Giggling, she added, "We can pretend that we are eating the entire gingerbread house. Besides, we need to do something while we wait for *Mutter* and *Opa* to come home."

Shrugging his shoulders, Andreas began, "Once upon a time…"

Mutter and *Opa* finally came home, and the family shared their meager dinner. Soon Josie snuggled under warm quilts between her mother and her brother, with *Oma* and *Opa* nearby, and drifted off. *Mutter*'s scream startled her awake. Rubbing the sleep from her eyes, she blinked and saw two soldiers pushing through the squeaking stall door with their rifles raised. One of them hit *Opa* in the head with the butt of his gun. *Opa*'s blood ran down his face and soaked into his shirt. Wurtz *Oma* pleaded, "Don't shoot him! Don't shoot him!" as they dragged *Opa* from the stall.

Josie felt her mother yank her off the straw bed and draw her into the shadows. She wondered if she was having another bad dream. Wurtz *Oma* was screaming and sobbing. Josie couldn't see *Opa* anymore. Her eyes darted around as she realized Andreas was gone, too. She clung to her mother and prayed. Squeezing her eyes tightly shut, she hoped she would wake up soon and the angry shouting would stop. Everything was happening so fast!

Mutter's grip tightened around Josie as one of the guards reached for her. *Mutter* screamed, "Get away from my child!" Her sobs turned to a sorrowful wail as Josie was torn from her arms.

Once outside, Josie could see a crowd of people forming in the faint light. Kicking and screaming as loudly as she could, she cried for help. No one came to her rescue. The soldier grabbed her flailing arms with one hand and yanked her head back. Slapping her hard across the face, he picked her by the arm and tossed her into a wooden wagon. Dizzy, Josie forced herself to sit up, she could see *Mutter* at the open wagon gate and crawled toward it. A soldier stood with his gun pointed at *Mutter*, keeping her away from Josie. *Mutter* was weeping, her arms tightly wrapped around Josie's cornhusk doll, mumbling words that didn't make sense.

Desperate to reach her mother, Josie tried to climb out past the soldier but was shoved back into the wagon. Then she realized Andreas was lying in a motionless heap on the wagon floor. Blood was dripping from a cut on his cheek and one eye was swollen shut. Thinking he was dead, she screamed and that's when she saw him move slightly.

Andreas rubbed the back of his hand across his mouth. Wiping blood on his sleeve, he tried to sit up. Josie was so thankful that her brother was alive that she hugged him, ignoring his cries of discomfort. "Andreas!" she sobbed into the side of his face, gripping him as tightly as she could. The wagon lurched forward, knocking them both against the wooden slats.

"Oh...!" he groaned.

"Shut up!" ordered one of the soldiers who rode a horse beside the wagon.

"Look," Andreas said, pointing toward a building. A cellar door was open, and *Opa* was struggling with two guards who were pushing him toward the opening. As the wagon drew near they could see that the cellar had water in it that reached up the steps.

"*Opa!*" Josie and Andreas yelled in unison. *Opa* stopped struggling and gave them a thumbs-up sign as the wagon pulled around the corner and out of sight.

Confused, Josie turned her tear-stained face to Andreas. "Why did *Opa* do that?"

The soldier on the horse was scowling in their direction. Andreas didn't want to draw his attention. Leaning close to Josie's ear, he whispered, "Because he wanted us to know he is going to be OK."

Following her brother's lead, Josie struggled to keep her voice low. "Andreas, what are we going to do now?"

Sighing heavily, he leaned back against the wagon's backboard. After several moments, he said, "We'll pray that everyone is OK, and when we get a chance, we'll escape and find *Mutter* again."

Josie wiped her arm across her eyes and scooted her bare feet up under her torn dress. Folding her hands on her lap, she bowed her head and began to pray. *Oma* always said that when God was in your life nothing was hopeless. She hoped her grandmother was right.

CHAPTER 10

Train to Rudolfsgnad, Yugoslavia, 1946

• • •

JOSIE DIDN'T KNOW HOW LONG she had been on the train, but she knew her legs were tired. There were so many people crowded into the cattle car that everyone had to stand. Her stomach ached terribly, so she tried to focus on something besides her gnawing hunger. Rubbing her eyes with the back of her hand, she pressed her face against the wooden planks and tried to ignore the rumbling of the boxcars as they moved down the tracks. She watched houses and fields rush by as the train moved further and further away from her family. When the train began to slow, she saw a church that reminded her of Saint Anna's in Glogon, but the tower on this one had been bombed. They came to a stop with such a jolt that it caused people to slam against one another. Struggling to keep her balance, Josie tried to keep from being pressed into the wall. She cried out as someone stepped on her foot. She hoped the guards would let them out soon. Shifting her weight from one foot to another, she tried not to think about how badly she needed to find an outhouse.

"Where are we?" she wondered out loud.

"This is Rudolfsgnad. It's an extermination camp," whispered the elderly woman next to her before throwing up. The vomit splattered on the slats of the wall. Gagging, Josie turned her face away from the smell.

She would ask Andreas what *extermination* meant as soon as he found her. The last time she saw him, just a few days ago, the guards were restraining him on the ground. One of them had forced his boot down on Andreas's chest, and was laughing cruelly. She had tried to reach her brother, but was forcefully thrown onto the train. She had banged and pulled on the door until her hands bled, but it was bolted shut from the outside. Before long the train began to move. Josie knew her brother would find her because he was good at finding people. She reminded herself that he and she had escaped from the Franzfeld camp and returned to their hometown two times in the past. He had gotten them safely to *Mutter* and *Oma* through each long, dangerous journey. Wrapping her arms around herself, she closed her eyes tightly and began repeating, "Andreas will find me. Andreas will find me."

Trembling, Josie remembered the terror of the second time they had been discovered. She and Andreas had returned to Glogon just as they had that first time. This time they were caught when Wurtz *Oma* had been picking beans in the garden. One of the fieldworkers had led the Serbian soldiers to the garden gate. Josie closed her eyes tightly and pressed her hands over her ears as if to block the memory of Wurtz *Oma*'s screams, but they were as clear as they had been that day. *Oma* pleaded with the soldiers, but they thrust the butts of their rifles into her back, forcing her toward the cow stall where the children hid. Sobbing, *Oma* collapsed to the ground. Josie cried. She kept stretching her arms toward *Oma*, but could only grab at the air as the soldiers lifted her toward the awaiting wagon. Andreas had tried to help *Oma* to her feet, but the soldiers grabbed him, throwing him into the wagon as if he were weightless. "Please, God, let *Oma* be OK," Josie sniveled into the over-crowded boxcar. She wiped her nose on the torn clothing that covered her thin arms.

The pain in her legs reminded her where she was now. Leaning her head against the wall, she tried to stretch her legs, but it was so hard to move. She lifted one bare foot and wiggled her toes while putting all her weight on the other foot; then she switched feet carefully so that no one stepped on them. Exhausted, she wondered when the heavy doors would be pulled open and they would be able to go outside and breathe in fresh air. Time dragged on until the sun went down, but still nobody came to let them out.

"Be still child," grumbled the woman next to her.

"I'm sorry. My legs are so tired, and it's so hot and stinky in here it's hard to breathe. We've been stopped for a very long time. When will they let us out?"

"Maybe never," sighed the woman. "Say your prayers, little one."

Fighting back tears, Josie turned her face away again. She wished that she could move away from this woman. She could hear several women and children crying throughout the crowded cattle car. One of the children sobbed, "I didn't mean to; I couldn't hold it anymore." A foul smell filled the train car. Gagging, Josie covered her nose. An elderly woman was throwing up at the other end of the crowded car. Josie couldn't hold it anymore and cried out as she felt the warm urine begin to run down her own legs. Embarrassed, she hung her head.

People began to fall into one another as the night went on and on. Someone yelled, "Oh, God! She's dead!" Josie's lower lip quivered as tears trickled down her face. Trying to keep her legs from shaking, she leaned against the wall in front of her. She breathed deeply and was able to pull in a tiny bit of the fresh air as she pressed her nose between the gaps in the slats. Again, she closed her eyes and prayed, "Dear God, please take care of me." As an afterthought she added, "Please take care of all of us." The woman in back of her leaned into Josie, supporting her arms on the wall above Josie's head. She didn't mind the body pressed against her back. Closing her eyes, she pretended that the woman behind her was *Mutter* with her arms wrapped around her. It seemed like such a long time since she had felt *Mutter* hold her. Standing very still, she tried not to do anything that would cause the woman to shift her weight away, and whispered, "I want my *Mutter*!"

Suddenly, the door was jerked open with a harsh clang. The early morning light and fresh air flooded in, startling the group. "Everyone get out! Now!" barked a guard. No one moved. "Get out now!" he shouted as he grabbed women and children by their arms or hair and flung them to the ground. Josie hurried to the edge, and an elderly woman reached for her so that she wouldn't fall.

"Thank you." Josie looked up into the woman's faded blue eyes.

Holding her hand out, the woman said, "Come and stand with me, child." Quickly Josie grabbed the woman's hand and took her place in a long line. Other cars were opened, and orders were shouted. People prayed or cried or watched in helpless disbelief as they waited.

Looking around, Josie was shocked to see houses without window shutters or doors. Hours passed as they waited in line. The summer sun baked down on her head. Her throat was dry; she couldn't remember when she had last had anything to eat or drink. There were trees, but many had missing leaves or cut-off branches.

Tugging on her new friend's arm, she asked, "What happened to the trees?"

The woman whispered, "I think people had to use the branches for cooking fuel."

Looking more closely, Josie noticed that there wasn't a blade of grass or a weed anywhere. A small child walked out of one of the doors in a nearby house and sat on the wooden steps. The child sobbed, hiding swollen eyes with her thin arms. Josie watched in horror as two guards dragged a woman's naked body through the doorway and threw her into a nearby wagon on top of several other bodies. Turning quickly, she buried her face in the frayed dress of her new friend and silently prayed, "Please, God, let my brother find me soon."

CHAPTER 11

Another Oma

• • •

STARTLED AWAKE, JOSIE SAT UP and squinted into the darkness, trying to make out the other images in the room. She could hear scurrying across the floor as the rats scratched about in the straw. One of the old women was taking her turn staying awake to guard the children so the hungry rats would not bite them. Shivering, Josie moved closer to the old woman lying next to her.

"You can call me *Oma* if you want to," the gentle woman told Josie one afternoon. "You miss your *Mutter* and I miss my little ones. I'm sure your real *Oma* won't mind." Neither of them had family in the Rudolfsgnad death camp, so they agreed to take care of each other.

Josie's new *Oma* had been trying to keep her from getting any weaker. Josie could feel the fleas and lice moving all over her as she tried to sleep on the hard floor. She listened to the comforting sound of *Oma*'s soft snoring. "How can *anyone* possibly sleep?" she wondered. Many of Josie's bites had turned into red blisters and infected sores, causing her to wince as she rubbed her arms. Stirring, *Oma* scolded her, pulling Josie's hands away from her skin, "Don't scratch, little one." But they itched so much that it was really hard to leave them alone; as soon as Josie heard the old woman's breathing shift back to snores she dug her fingers into her raw skin once more.

Where is Andreas? she thought. She wanted to take her new *Oma* back to Glogon to meet her family. Comforted by the thought, she fell back to sleep.

The next morning Josie crawled through the open doorway of the house and sat on the step of the small dwelling she and *Oma* now shared with twenty-five other people. The fleas weren't as bad outside as they were inside, and the smell was much better. She watched *Oma* in the yard setting up a box in the dirt. Sometimes *Oma* was able to catch a bird that flew into the yard by saving some of the dry cornbread that came with the watered down soup they got once a day if the guards weren't in a bad mood.

"Please God, let her catch a bird today," Josie prayed. A bird would mean they would have meat tonight. *Oma* bent over and propped up one end of the box with a stick. She tied a long piece of string to the bottom of the stick and placed a few morsels of dry bread under the box. When *Oma* looked up, Josie smiled and waved.

Oma walked toward Josie and held out the string. "Would you like to pull the string when a bird flies under the box to eat the crumbs?"

"What if I miss?" worried Josie, not feeling confident she could react as quickly as the bird.

"Sometimes that happens," answered *Oma*, "How about if we hold it together? Then we can both catch our meal." Leaning forward, she patted Josie's scabbed knee. "Did you walk to the step this morning?"

Hanging her head, Josie answered, "No. It hurts too much and I'm too tired."

Her new *Oma* wrapped her arm around Josie's bony shoulders and pulled her close. "Josie, you have to keep trying to walk or your legs will stop working," she rebuked.

"Look." Being glad to have a reason to change the subject, Josie pointed cautiously toward the bird that was pecking at the tidbits under the box.

Oma placed the end of the string in Josie's frail hand. Placing her own bony fingers over the top of Josie's, she whispered, "OK. Get ready. Now!"

"*Oma!* We did it!" Josie laughed and clapped in excitement.

Dust puffed up around the edges as the small wooden crate dropped to the ground, capturing the startled bird. Josie knew this was going to be a good day. She couldn't wait until *Oma* started to cook their dinner.

A small fire needed to be built in order to cook the bird; Josie watched as Oma hobbled through the sparse yard looking for anything that might be left to use for fuel. Some of the doors and all of the window shutters had been burned before they had arrived in this awful place; and the soldiers had taken the furniture long ago. Any leaves that had sprouted on the branches this spring had been eaten, and the lower branches that were within reach had been broken off for firewood long ago.

Josie's forehead furrowed with worry as she called out, "*Oma*, what if we can't find anything to burn?"

"Come, child," *Oma* said. She helped Josie to her feet and supported her as they made their way to the trap. "You sit here," *Oma* said as she plopped Josie on the crate that covered the trapped bird. "I'll find something to burn. Don't worry about building fires; if we have to, we'll burn our box."

"No, *Oma*!" Josie replied with alarm. "If we burn our box we won't be able to catch another bird."

"Don't worry, little one. I'll find something to burn," said *Oma*. Josie wasn't sure that was going to be possible as she followed her friend's glances around the barren yard. A few moments later, Oma's shoulders slumped forward as she said, "Sit on the box and keep our bird safe. I'll be right back."

Sitting very still, Josie watched as *Oma* walked up to one of the guards. She tried very hard to hear what they were saying, but they had their voices lowered and were too far away. She watched *Oma* disappear behind a small building. Josie felt her heart pounding inside her chest as she worried that the guard wouldn't let *Oma* come back to her. Time passed slowly as she sat. She could hear the bird moving around beneath her. Concerned that *Oma* might need her; she began to wonder if she should try to walk to the building. "Please let *Oma* come back soon," she pleaded.

Josie turned to look back at the house when she heard a woman sobbing. Guards were carrying three more bodies through the front door and over to the waiting death wagon. She watched as they heaved the dead bodies on top of the already full wagon. Their twisted bodies looked like broken dolls. Every day the wagons were piled high with naked women and children who had died in the night. Their clothing was very valuable in a place where people had so little. Covering her eyes, Josie lowered her head. The lump in her throat told her that her body wanted to cry, but the tears didn't come.

After what seemed like a long time, she forced herself to look up again; she was so relieved to see her new *Oma* walking toward her carrying pieces of a broken chair. *Oma* had tears in her eyes, and Josie wondered if she too had seen the bodies being removed. Struggling to stand on wobbly legs she waited anxiously. The moment *Oma* was in reach Josie wrapped her arms around *Oma*'s waist and hung on tightly. *Oma* seemed a little unsteady herself, as the two of them got ready to build the fire.

"Are you OK, *Oma*?" Josie asked, but *Oma* didn't answer. Josie watched carefully as *Oma* went about the business of trying to remove the bird from the trap without letting it get away. She smiled in anticipation of the few bites of meat they were going to eat. It had been a long time since they had such a feast.

Later that night, Josie woke up aching with a high fever. *Oma* washed her sweaty face with cool water and prayed for her. Josie tried to talk, but she didn't have the strength. She drifted in and out of consciousness. She awoke once and overheard her new *Oma* ask someone to beg one of the death wagon drivers to get a message to Josie's brother, Andreas, about how ill she was when the driver next drove through the Franzfeld camp.

Frightened that this meant she was dying, Josie whimpered, "*Oma*, don't let them take my dress away. Please, don't let them take my dress away when they take my body." It was the dress that her real *Oma* and *Mutter* had made for her. She kept trying to tell *Oma*, but she didn't seem to understand. She just kept saying, "It will be OK, little one. God is with you."

Sometimes when Josie woke up she was confused and thought her new *Oma* was *Mutter*. *Oma* tried to get Josie to swallow a small amount of thin barley soup, but it was too difficult. Most of the liquid ran out of her mouth and onto the floor. Josie felt bad about wasting the small amount of soup the guards provided, but mostly she worried about them taking away her dress with the special pocket *Mutter* had sewn just for her.

CHAPTER 12

Blood in the Snow

● ● ●

BLINKING SEVERAL TIMES, JOSIE WHISPERED, "*Mutter*, you found me." This time she was not dreaming. Now she was certain that *Mutter* had gotten her new *Oma's* message about Josie being very ill. Her mother had walked several miles to Rudolfsgnad to find her. Smiling weakly, Josie fell back into a restless sleep.

Sores broke open on Josie's back as *her mother* gently ran her hand over her skin. *Mutter's* voice cracked as she whispered, "As soon as you are strong enough we are going to escape from this horrible place and join the rest of the family." Josie couldn't imagine how *Mutter* had managed to sneak into Rudolfsgnad past all of the armed guards without being killed, and she had no idea how they could possibly get out. *Mutter* just kept saying, "God will help us find a way."

"It's so far," she said, struggling to keep her eyes open. Losing the battle, she dreamed of the two earlier escapes from Franzfeld with Andreas and of sleeping in the snow. Visions of angry soldiers ripping her from *Mutter*'s arms kept wandering in and out of her mind as she slept fitfully.

The next time she opened her eyes, she could hear *Mutter* and her new *Oma* whispering, but she couldn't make out the words. The winter sun was shining faintly through the open window; squinting through her swollen eyelids, she tried to locate her mother in the room. She brightened when she remembered they were going home. Finally her new *Oma* could meet her family.

"Ah, you're awake." *Mutter* gently kissed her cheek. "You must try to eat something." Her mother fed her soup made from a few small potatoes she had hidden in the hem of her dress. It was possible to glean a few after the harvest, and *Mutter* had been careful not to get caught.

"It smells so good." Josie's mouth watered with anticipation. "I love potatoes."

The next day *Mutter* fed her more soup and one of the eggs she had taken from the chicken coup she had discovered at a farm on her journey to rescue Josie.

Mutter carried Josie as she and *Oma* walked along the side of the house to a tall tree with dormant branches that were too high for anyone to reach. *Mutter* found a sunny place, and she propped Josie up next to the tree. Her legs felt stronger and she was able to stand for short periods of time.

Turning to *Oma*, *Mutter* said, "We are going to leave tonight as soon as it gets dark."

Josie smiled from ear to ear. She grabbed *Oma*'s arms for support and giggled, "I can't wait for you to meet everyone. They are going to really like you." Her smile fell as she saw the tears well up in *Oma*'s eyes. She didn't understand. "*Oma*, don't worry. They will like you, and you are going to like them, too."

"My child," said *Oma*. "I am not going to be able to go with you."

"But you have to go!" insisted Josie.

"Shhhh," said *Oma*, looking around hesitantly. The old woman kneeled and looked lovingly into Josie's eyes. "Now listen. I am too old to travel as far as you are going. I would only slow you down."

Josie burst into tears. "No, *Oma*! I can't leave you. I just can't!" Whipping around she pleaded, "*Mutter*, please tell her. Tell her that she has to come with us."

Josie's mother pulled her close and spoke softly while stroking what was left of her little girl's matted hair. "Honey, I don't want to leave your new *Oma* either. She took such good care of you, and she is like family. No, she is family." Swallowing hard, *Mutter* continued. "But she's right. She won't be able to make the trip. It would be too hard on her."

"*Mutter* we can't leave her. We can't!" Josie sat down in the dirt and buried her face in her hands.

Oma bent down and placed a weathered hand on either side of Josie's face. She looked straight into Josie's tearstained eyes and forced a smile. Clearing her throat she said, "I want you to listen to me carefully. I will always be with you, Josie. When you love someone, they are always in your heart." She gently placed a gnarled hand on Josie's chest. "Did you hear me? I will always be in your heart, and you will always be in mine. Do you understand, little one?"

Josie's lower lip trembled. "But, *Oma*, what if I never see you again?" Her heart felt like it was breaking.

Oma knelt in the dirt. Pulling Josie close to her, she gently placed her hand against Josie's chest. "Remember, I'll always be in your heart. Tell me you understand." Josie tried to use her voice, but her throat hurt too much. She nodded her head and wrapped her arms around *Oma*.

The sun slipped slowly away as clouds began to build, and soon snow drifted down on them. *Mutter* helped *Oma* get up from the dirt, and then she picked Josie up. The three of them made their way back to the house.

They hoped they would get a ration of cracked corn today. When it came, *Oma* gave *Mutter* her small portion. "I'm not hungry tonight, Rosalia. You are going to need all of the strength you have with what's ahead of you."

Mutter smiled gratefully. "God bless you."

In the evening the three of them said their prayers together.

"Good night," *Mutter* said before going to speak with the mother of another family that was planning to escape with them. Olga had made the dangerous trip from Glogon to Rudolfsgnad with *Mutter* in hopes of rescuing her two girls who lived in another house in the camp.

Josie snuggled next to *Oma* on the hard floor. She could feel *Oma*'s arms wrapped around her and her warm, comforting breath on the back of her neck. "I will always remember my new *Oma*," thought Josie as she drifted off to sleep.

The clouds covered the moon, making the sky dark as they quietly snuck out of the house and across the dirt yard several hours before sunrise on the morning of the planned escape. Josie was too weak to walk in the deepening snow, so *Mutter* carried her on her back. New *Oma* had wrapped Josie's feet in rags for warmth. Olga and her two girls were making the frightening journey with them.

They hid between two buildings, waiting for the exact moment when the guards turned to patrol in the opposite direction. "Now!" *Mutter* whispered. They had only a few minutes to make it under the wire fence and reach the cover of the forest beyond, so they ran with all their strength. It wasn't an easy task for two women with three young children.

Safely in the trees, *Mutter* and Olga collapsed in the dense shadows to catch their breath. Everyone knew there must be no noise.

They hadn't stopped long when *Mutter* said, "We must go now. We must get as far from here as we can." They pushed on silently through the snow.

"*Mutter*, how did you know Olga would want to come with us?" Josie softly whispered into her mother's ear.

"Olga has been trying to find her girls the way I have been looking for you," *Mutter* replied.

Josie shivered from the cold as she pressed up against *Mutter*'s back. She watched the two little girls ahead of them shaking as they held their mother's hand. "Will we travel all night?" she asked. She was glad they still had shoes. The snow was deeper here and they struggled through each arduous step.

"We must use the darkness to travel and use the day to hide and rest," *Mutter* answered breathlessly.

Olga pulled her two girls close to her. "Rosalia, I don't know how much farther we can walk in this. We need to find a place to stop for the night."

Mutter sounded stern, "We can't stop. When the sun comes up we need to be as far away as possible."

Josie heard a twig snap and guards shouting as they surrounded the little group of women and children. She gasped as one of the soldiers shoved Olga down and tore her dress. "You filthy woman!" he shouted. "Where do you think you are going?"

Olga's two daughters clung to their mother. Josie and *Mutter* watched in horror as the guards swiftly shot Olga and her children.

"No! No!" Josie screamed repeatedly as the guards kept shooting. The bodies bounced, making strange movements as the bullets hit them. *Mutter* let Josie slip from her back and stood firmly in front of her. Clinging to *Mutter*'s dress, Josie struggled to stand. She peered at the three lifeless bodies as their blood soaked into the snow. A red outline formed around them and grew fuzzy as the scarlet color seeped around the motionless bodies lying on what was now an icy grave. Everything seemed to move in slow motion as the guards turned and pointed their guns at Josie and *Mutter*. Josie's weak legs collapsed, and she dropped to her knees. Her entire body began shaking. She could see the hateful faces of the guards and knew they were screaming, but all she could hear was *Mutter* saying over and over again, "My God, protect us. My God, protect us. My God, protect us."

A guard with a mustache hit *Mutter* across the face with the butt of his gun, knocking her into the snow beside Josie. Just as he swung his gun back to hit her a second time, another guard stepped between them. He yelled, "No! We will take them back to Rudolfsgnad. They can tell the others that this is what happens to those who try to escape." Josie was yanked to her feet. The guard pulled away in disgust when a boil on Josie's arm burst open with his rough grip. Wiping the puss on his pants, he ordered them to walk back the way they had come. *Mutter* picked Josie up and slowly carried her back the way they had come. *Mutter*'s mouth was bleeding and her face began to swell, but they were alive.

The sun was high in the sky as Josie and *Mutter* were marched back through the barbed wire fence of the camp. *Mutter* sat Josie down just inside their doorway and slid to the floor. She burst into tears as Josie's new *Oma* rushed to them. "Thank God you are OK," *Oma* exclaimed as she wrapped her arms around Josie and covered her with kisses. The three of them sat on the floor without speaking for a long time.

After the food ration that evening, *Mutter* told *Oma* about Olga and her two little girls being murdered in the snow. "Rosalia, just thank God that you two were saved. Maybe you are meant to stay here."

Glancing at Josie, *Mutter* said softly, "Josie will not live if we stay. We will leave again tonight."

Shocked, Josie's voice trembled. "What if they shoot us?"

"They could shoot us as we sit here if they want. They will not expect us to try to leave again so soon. We'll leave tonight."

Touching *Mutter*'s split and swollen lip, *Oma* said, "Rosalia, you are not strong enough. You should rest. It's too soon to try this again."

Mutter looked at Josie and *Oma* and said firmly, "We'll rest until the middle of the night, and then we will leave. I'm taking Josie home."

Oma protested, "Rosalia, you are not in the right state of mind to make this decision. Look outside; it will be snowing again by then. It will be even more difficult to walk."

Mutter's voice sounded weak as she struggled to answer, "If it is God's will that it snows, that is OK. It will cover our footsteps."

Early the next morning, Josie watched the snow falling heavily as they slipped from camp. "*Oma* was right. It is snowing again," she said. She hoped *Mutter* would also be right and that the snow would cover their footprints. No matter how tightly her mother held her, she couldn't stop shaking.

CHAPTER 13

Journey to Freedom, 1947

• • •

Josie sat up, rubbed her eyes, and stretched. Looking around in disbelief, she saw the smiling faces of Andreas, *Mutter*, Wurtz *Oma*, and Wurtz *Opa*.

"Where are we?" she whispered. If she was only dreaming, she didn't want to wake up.

Mutter was the first to answer. "We're in Glogon. We arrived several days ago. You have been asleep most of the time." *Mutter's* voiced cracked as she continued: "Your fever was so high I thought we were going to lose you." She pulled Josie into her arms, her eyes brimming with tears. "I was so afraid, but look at you. God took care of you. There is color in your face, and your brown eyes are sparkling again."

Sitting up again, Josie gasped as she looked down at the crusty patches of skin covering her body. "I look so ugly," she said through sobs.

Wurtz *Oma* sat down next to her. "You look beautiful. You are alive."

"I don't want to be alive!" sobbed Josie.

"Stop that right now!" ordered Wurtz *Oma* in a quiet but firm voice. "It is a sin to talk that way. You must be thankful to be alive. Wurtz *Opa* had to lance the boils on your body. These are just scabs. They will heal." Everyone bent over to hug Josie, being careful not to put pressure on the tender sores.

After the excitement was over, Wurtz *Opa* stood and faced everyone in the stall. "As soon as Josie is strong enough, we must leave. Every day we delay, we risk being caught hiding the children," he said. "Anna and Rosalia, you need to hide away as many vegetables and eggs as you think we can carry. We won't let this family be separated again." Placing his hand on Andreas's shoulder, he lowered his voice. "Josie is alive because you escaped Franzfeld to bring word to us about her. It was a terrible risk, but you are a courageous young man. We are all so proud of you. Soon, I will need you to find Trollmann *Oma* and tell her how to join us. Then we will leave Yugoslavia forever."

Andreas looked doubtful. "Where will we go, *Opa?* How will *Vater* find us?"

"We will go to Austria where they will not hate us for being German." Wurtz *Opa* bent down and picked up a piece of straw from the bedding that Josie lie on. He broke the straw in his hand. "Maybe we will travel to America. We have relatives there. You know, Andreas, your *Vater* was born in America when your Trollmann *Oma* and *Opa* were there long ago. First, we must find safety. Then we will find a way to get word to your *Vater.*"

Josie tried to sit up. "I didn't know that *Vater* was born in America. What is it like there?"

Wurtz *Oma* gave *Opa* a stern look as she nudged Josie back under the covers. "This is enough talk. If we have such big plans, Josie needs to rest."

Over the next few weeks, Josie watched *Oma* and *Mutter* hide potatoes, onions, and eggs in two cloth bags hanging behind the tools in the stall. Sometimes Josie would watch *Oma* through the slats of wood from her hiding place in the animal shed. When *Oma* was weeding the garden or hanging the clothes she washed for the Serbs who lived in the house, she would place a small vegetable inside her apron pockets, or in the hole she had made inside the hem of her dress. Gradually, their little supply began to grow.

One night, Josie woke up to the sound of *Opa* talking to someone. As she squinted into the darkness, she realized that it was Trollmann *Oma*. She had not seen her Trollmann *Oma* since the day she and Andreas were taken to Franzfeld the first time. She wanted to give her a big hug, but knew that if she let them know that she was awake, their conversation would change. Trollmann *Oma* was holding a cloth sack similar to the ones *Mutter* and Wurtz *Oma* had been filling with food. Smiling, Trollmann *Oma* opened the bag. "Look, Johann, I was able to get this chunk of smoked bacon from a wagon this morning."

Opa frowned. "Ursula, you should not have taken such a big risk. They might have killed you!"

Through half-closed eyelids, Josie watched Trollmann *Oma* cross her arms and take a defiant stance. *Oh, no!* she thought, Oma *is going to argue with* Opa.

Josie was relieved to see *Opa* lean forward and place his hand on Trollmann *Oma*'s bent shoulder. Quickly he said, "Thank you. We are blessed to have such a fine piece of meat in our possession as we begin our journey. Anna and I thank God you were not caught."

Josie couldn't wait another second. Being careful not to wake Andreas and *Mutter,* who slept beside her, she hurriedly tiptoed over to Trollmann *Oma* and threw her arms around her.

"*Oma,* I've missed you!" Josie whispered louder than she had intended.

Tears ran down Trollmann *Oma*'s face as she pulled Josie closer to her. "And I've missed you, little one." Pulling away, she placed a hand on either side of Josie's face and kissed her forehead. "I heard that you were very ill, but look at you. You are a beautiful sight."

"I'm feeling so much better, *Oma. Mutter* and Wurtz *Oma* have been taking care of me."

Trollmann *Oma* smiled as she glanced at her exhausted loved ones. "I see they have been doing a good job. *Liebling,*

I think you should rest. We have a lot of traveling ahead of us, and you are going to need your strength."

Josie giggled as *Mutter* and Wurtz *Oma* both got up. Andreas awakened next, rubbing the sleep from his eyes. "Trollmann *Oma*, is that really you?"

Wurtz *Opa* threw up his hands in frustration. "OK, if everyone is getting up, we should leave within the hour." After he gave instructions to everyone else, he turned to Josie. "I want you to sit quietly and save your energy." Glaring in *Opa*'s direction, she crossed her arms. *Opa* seemed in a bad mood, so Josie decided not to tell him what she thought about saving her energy. Instead, she moved to the far wall and tried to stay out of the way as she watched Wurtz *Oma* place their old, chipped cooking pot into a sack.

They left quietly, under the cover of a moonless night, and walked through the chilly darkness into the next day. They hid in cornfields and vineyards, or took cover in dense woodlands when they could. Josie's body felt weak and exhausted as she fought to keep up with the others. "*Opa*, I'm so tired. Can we sit down for just a little while?"

Opa leaned over and picked Josie up. "Not far from here there is a train that will be leaving for the next town. We will try to jump onto one of the cattle cars while it is moving slowly. Then we will have time to rest."

Stiffening Josie remembered the last time she was in a cattle car. "*Opa*, what if it takes us somewhere bad?

He responded, "I won't let that happen." Josie wrapped her arms around her grandfather's neck, placed her head against his shoulder and closed her eyes. The next thing she remembered, *Opa* was running with her in his arms. Reaching up, he passed her to *Mutter*, who was standing in an empty boxcar on a moving train. Josie watched in horror as he fought to keep up with the train. He was breathless when he finally pulled himself aboard with the rest of the family.

Once everyone was seated in the boxcar, *Oma* and *Mutter* cut chunks of smoked bacon and apples for everyone.

"Where will this train take us?" Andreas asked.

"Closer to Hungary," *Opa* answered. "We'll be safer when we reach the Hungarian border. It will be less dangerous to travel through Hungary into Austria."

Suddenly feeling very hungry, Josie shoved her portion into her mouth and reached out her hand. "May I have more please?" she asked.

Mutter's eyes filled with tears as she kissed her daughter's open hand. "We need to make the food we have last. You will get more tomorrow."

"Here, take mine," offered Trollmann *Oma*. "We will find a farmhouse with people who will give us a piece of bread and a slice of meat. Just wait and see. God will open the hearts of the Hungarian people."

Several nights later, *Opa* came back to their camp with a satchel full of food he had gotten from a nearby house, and *Oma* made a delicious stew. Josie lay back on the soft green grass with a full stomach, and watched her mother and grandmothers visiting around the small cooking fire they had made. She was happy *Opa* could speak a bit of Hungarian. Josie smiled and turned to Andreas, "Trollmann *Oma* was right. Things are better here. I wish *Opa* wasn't in such a hurry to cross the border into Austria."

Andreas frowned. "Josie, *Opa* knows what he is doing. He said we are still not safe. He is going to help us go all the way to America."

"I know," she sighed. "It's just hard to walk all the time. I'm tired."

"If you don't want to get caught and sent back to the camp, we have to keep going," snapped Andreas. "Quit complaining, *Opa* said we might have another fifty miles before we reach Austria's border. It might even be more!"

Josie narrowed her eyes, crossed her arms and glared at her brother.

It wasn't long before *Opa* rounded everyone up and they continued walking toward Austria. I hope *Opa* knows where he is going," thought Josie as she pushed her tired legs closer to the forest that she was told lay ahead of them. Squinting, she couldn't see anything in front of them that looked like a forest to her.

When they finally reached the tall, thick, trees, Josie struggled to catch up to *Mutter.* The trees were so close together that it was hard to see the stars in the sky anymore.

"Stand still!" *Opa* whispered urgently.

Mutter and Josie ran into the back of Wurtz *Oma* as the small group came to a sudden stop. Standing bunched together in the deep, black forest, Josie could hear twigs snapping in the distance. *"Mutter,* what is that noise?" Josie's legs began to tremble as she imagined angry soldiers with loaded guns making their way through the trees toward them.

"Shhh," *Mutter* whispered as she gently picked her up.

She remembered the warning the soldier had given her and *Mutter* when they got caught trying to escape from Rudolfsgnad the first time. Her stomach tightened as she pictured the crimson blood on the snow.

Suddenly, soldiers carrying guns burst through the trees, surrounding them. Josie screamed. She felt her mother's arms tighten around her possessively, and she thought she heard someone far away tell her to be quiet, but she couldn't stop the piercing cry that was deep inside of her.

CHAPTER 14

Crossing Europe, Fall 1947–1949

• • •

JOSIE CLUNG TIGHTLY TO *MUTTER* as the family huddled in the dark forest. Her voice was gone and the only sound she heard was her heart pounding in her ears as they waited.

After what seemed like a long, long silence, one of the Russian border guards yelled out in broken German, "Don't move. Don't be afraid. We'll help you!" Josie could see that *Opa* didn't trust the soldiers, but they had little choice but to obey. After a brief discussion, the soldiers led them to housing for refugees in the Soviet Occupied Zone of Austria.

Once again, they found themselves in a camp. Fortunately this was not like the two previous concentration camps that Josie had been in, it was a camp for displaced persons. The food was better and it was easier to stay clean. There were also no fences, and the soldiers were only a little mean. The six family members shared a small one-room house. During the day, Josie went to a school where everyone spoke German. She was seven years old now, and she had never been to school before. Andreas, who was now fifteen, traveled with the adults on a wagon to work on the farms every day.

"I have a new friend!" she told *Mutter* when she came home from school the first day. "Katherine knows how to read."

"You will read soon, Josie," *Mutter* told her. "You are smart and will learn quickly." Sometimes after school Josie and Katherine sat in the branches of an old pear tree, holding a book. Josie was enjoying school and starting to feel safe at this new camp. She liked school and she had friends. The Edelweiss flowers were beautiful as they bloomed. Sometimes she even forgot about the ill-tempered guards.

One evening while Josie was sweeping the porch for *Mutter*, she could hear Wurtz *Oma* and *Opa* talking.

"We are no better than slaves," Wurtz *Opa* complained to *Oma*. "We work all day without pay. Are we supposed to be thankful they don't break our ribs with their rifle butts?"

"We are together, Johann, and we have food," *Oma* said.

Opa continued to grumble as he placed a pile of wood beside the stove. "We may no longer be in jeopardy of being killed every day, but we are still in forced labor."

Josie came bouncing into the kitchen and gave *Opa* a big hug. "Things are better here, *Opa*. I have my friend, Katherine, to play with, and Trollmann *Oma* says I am putting meat on my bones." She twirled around and gave *Opa* a big smile.

"If you are so big and strong, you can help me bring more wood inside," *Opa* replied. "Andreas, you can bring *Oma* some water." They both got up to follow *Opa*, and he put an arm around each of them.

When Josie returned to the kitchen with an armload of wood, Wurtz *Oma* and Trollmann *Oma* were standing near the stove whispering to *Mutter.*

"What's for dinner?" she asked, wondering why they had stopped talking so suddenly. Wurtz *Oma* turned away from the pot of lentil soup she was stirring and passed the wooden spoon to *Mutter.*

Grabbing Josie's hand, *Oma* said, "Let's go find *Opa* and Andreas. I think they're on the porch. It's almost time for dinner."

Wurtz *Oma* rushed her quickly through the room, hurting Josie's arm as she was pulled across the floor. The only words she could understand were when Trollmann *Oma* whispered to *Mutter*, "…leave tonight."

Josie's throat tightened as she yanked her hand free and ran to *Opa*. Jumping into his lap, she wrapped her arms tightly around his neck, "Oh, *Opa*," she gasped.

"What's wrong, *Liebling*?" *Opa* asked, messing up her hair.

"We're not really leaving are we?" Pleading, Josie sat back and searched his eyes.

Opa looked past her at *Oma* and sighed. After what seemed like a long time, he cleared his throat and said, "Josie, we are not free here. I know you don't want to leave your new friend, but if we are going to be safe we need to go to the American occupation zone. They will help us travel to our relatives in the United States."

Andreas hurried across the small porch to where *Opa* sat with Josie in his lap. "I'm ready to go. When do we leave?"

"Tonight," answered *Opa* as he pulled both Josie and Andreas into a big hug. "I have found a man who will show us the way through the mountains. We'll leave tonight."

"*Opa*, how will I say goodbye to Katherine?" Josie's brown eyes darkened as she chewed on her lower lip.

Opa looked away. *His* voice sounded tired. "You can't say goodbye, *Schatzie*. No one can know we are leaving, because it would put us in danger."

Josie ran into the house. She threw herself onto the pallet that served as her bed and buried her face in her arms.

The next few days were hard. Josie didn't talk to anyone as they climbed through the Austrian mountains. Not that anyone seemed to notice. She hated sneaking into strangers' barns to sleep, but it was even scarier when they had to make a bed in the open forest. Along the journey to the American Occupation Zone Josie made a decision not to make new friends. Stomping through the thick trees, she thought about *Opa*'s plan to contact the American Embassy in Vienna and talk to them about helping her family im-migrate to the United States. She didn't know what "im-migrate" meant, but she was sure it involved leaving again.

Remembering her friend Katherine, she swallowed hard against the lump in her throat and vowed, "No new friends." If she didn't make friends at the new school, there would be no one to miss when she left for America.

Arriving at the Displaced Persons Camp in the American Occupation Zone, the family waited as *Mutter* checked with the Red Cross for news of *Vater*. When she returned, all hope seemed to have disappeared from her face.

"No word," was all *Mutter* said.

"We will check again soon, Rosalia." Trollmann *Oma* put her arm around *Mutter*'s shoulder. There was a long silence as they found shelter for the night. The look on her family members' faces left Josie wondering if she would ever see her father again. But she didn't ask.

This displaced persons camp had a school like the last one, but Josie remembered her decision and didn't make new friends. Sometimes she was lonely. She often read books or played alone with her cornhusk doll after school. One evening *Oma* was in the kitchen with her as she read.

"*Oma*, do you think Katherine is mad at me for leaving without saying goodbye?" She looked over at *Oma*, who sat near her at the kitchen table. Trollmann *Oma* was opening a package that had arrived from her sister in the United States.

"Look at this!" *Oma* interrupted Josie, as she pulled the third five-dollar bill from the middle of a flour sack. She held them up for all the family to see. *Oma's* eyes sparkled for the first time in a long while. "We will leave in the morning. This money came just in time for our voyage to America." Over the last few weeks *Oma* had discovered many little surprises in food packages from family members in America. Josie even had new shoes that came buried in a sack of sugar.

"Trollmann *Oma*, why is the money hidden in the flour sack?" she asked. "Why would anyone care if our family sends us money?"

Trollmann *Oma's* voice dropped to a whisper as she replied, "You never know who is looking at our mail. This is the only way that my sister and her husband can be sure that we will have enough money for our expenses when we travel." Looking at the piece of paper that *Oma* called money, Josie marveled at the strange writing and pictures. *Oma* gave Josie a tender smile as she kissed her cheek. "I can't wait for them to meet you and Andreas when we arrive in California."

"California!" exclaimed Josie. "I thought we were going to the United States."

Opa moved across the room to join them and picked Josie up in a giant bear hug as he swung her around. "California is one of the states in the United States of America, silly one. America is a very big place." Setting her down on the floor he patted the top of her head with his big hands. "Now you need to stop asking questions." *Opa* motioned for *Mutter*, and

Andreas to come closer. Clearing his throat he said, "This will be our last night together for a while." He paused to make eye contact with both Andreas and Josie. "The two of you are going to travel to America with your mom and Trollmann *Oma*. Wurtz *Oma* and I will come later." Josie started to protest, but *Opa* held up a finger to stop her. Suddenly his voice was firm. "We need to thank God for keeping us safe this far, and we must trust him to bring us all together again in what will be our new country. God willing, we will all become Americans."

Stepping between them, Andreas wrapped an arm around Wurtz *Opa* and Wurtz *Oma*. After what seemed like a long time, he said softly, "Why can't we wait and all go together? I don't want to go to America without the two of you." Josie thought his voice sounded strange—almost as though his throat was too tight for the words to come out. She hoped he wasn't getting sick.

"Let's not talk nonsense," replied *Opa*. "Besides, you will be with family in America by Christmas. We will only be separated a few months. We've applied for a visa, and your Great Uncle Joe and Aunt Mary will be sponsoring us soon. When we arrive in California, they will help us get to the city of Fresno. Then *Oma* and I will find you. I'm sure we'll be together again by Easter." *Opa* looked around the small circle, and clearing the husky sound from his throat he added, "Don't worry for a moment; we have come safely this far. God will bring our family together again."

Trollmann *Oma* looked at Josie and Andreas and smiled. "We are going to have a new home. Just think, by tomorrow night we will be in Paris, France. The Port of Cherbourg, where we meet our ship, is not far from Paris. Once we board the *Queen Mary*, we'll be on our way to New York, a great city in America."

"Is California near New York?" asked Andreas.

Trollmann *Oma* shook her head. "No. Someone from the American embassy there will help us get on a big bus that will take us the rest of the way to California. You are going to like America, Andreas. Your *Vater* liked it there when he was a boy."

"I just turned seventeen, *Oma*," retorted Andreas. "I'm not a boy anymore."

"No you're not," said Wurtz *Oma*. "Andreas, you are going to be the man of the family until *Opa* and I see you again." Tears filled Oma's eyes as she grabbed *Mutter* and hugged her tightly. "I can't wait to hear all about your voyage when we are together again." With that said, she kissed both Andreas and Josie, and patted Trollmann *Oma*'s shoulder as she and *Opa* wished them a safe journey.

Josie wasn't sure whether to be happy or sad. When she looked over at her mother she was pretty sure that she wasn't the only one who was confused. *Mutter* was mumbling words that didn't make sense again. Both of her grandmothers had told her that her mother was suffering from intense grief that would heal over time. She prayed that it would happen soon.

CHAPTER 15

Queen Mary to America, December 1949

• • •

THE WIND WHIPPED THROUGH JOSIE's short, honey-blond curls as her small fingers gripped the cold metal of the ship's railing. She giggled at the salty ocean spray as it flew up from the rolling expanse of dark water that surrounded the huge ship. Turning away from the sea, she noticed all of the people moving around the wooden decks. Josie wondered where they were headed, there were so many possibilities, they could be going to the pool, to play shuffle board, to see a movie, or maybe to eat at one of the restaurants. Grinning, she pictured their room as a tiny house and pretended they were on a floating town.

As they moved closer and closer to America, she thought about all of the wonderful things that she had experienced in the last couple of weeks. She had flown up in the sky on a small plane from Vienna, Austria, to Paris, France. It had been like being a bird flying in the air.

When they had arrived in Paris they were completely soaked by the rain as they struggled to reach their hotel. There had been a soft, clean bed and real electric lights. Smiling, Josie remembered being fascinated with the electricity as she stood on a chair and pulled the string that switched the lights on and off; that is, until *Mutter* scolded her. She and Andreas sneaked out of the hotel and ran down the street to see the Eiffel Tower while *Mutter* and *Oma* were napping. Boy, would they be in trouble if *Oma* ever found out.

Josie laughed out loud when she remembered Trollmann *Oma* slapping Andreas's hand away from the big bowl of fruit on the table. *Oma* had been afraid that they would be charged extra money if they ate anything in the room. She also hadn't wanted anyone to go beyond the hotel lobby, but one night *Mutter* talked her into taking everyone out to dinner at a French Restaurant with real waiters. "Let's eat out; just once," Josie's mother had begged her mother-in-law.

Oma had finally agreed, but warned that they must be very thrifty with their money. She kept repeating, "There will be no more packages with hidden surprises before we arrive in America."

Seeing Trollmann *Oma* walking toward her along the ship's deck brought Josie back to the present. Waving, she called out, "*Oma*, I was just remembering the look on the French waiter's face when you paid for our dinner with American money," she giggled.

Oma joined her in the laughter. "The waiter brought so much change that I didn't know where to put it all."

Giving *Oma* a quick hug, she asked, "Do you think *Mutter* will feel well enough to visit the shops on the ship tomorrow? Or maybe she could come out and sit by one of the pools? Andreas and I could even teach her how to play shuffleboard." *Mutter* had been throwing up since they got on the ship. She was weak, and Andreas had gone to take her some broth.

Oma shook her head. "I don't think so, Josie. She is pretty seasick. We must let her get some rest. Your *Mutter* will feel better when we are on dry land."

The black scarf Trollmann *Oma* wore on her head was whipping around in the wind as she struggled to retie it. As she was pulled into a hug, Josie's cheek rubbed against the rough fabric of *Oma*'s coat. Pulling her even closer, *Oma* said, "Just think! We are going to be in America in just a couple of days."

Josie thought her eyes might pop right out of her head. "*Oma*, do we really only have a couple of days left before we reach America?"

Smiling, Trollmann *Oma* answered, "Yes, child, it doesn't take long for such a big ship to cross the ocean."

Pulling her own black wool coat tightly against the cold, Josie searched the faces along the ship's second-class deck for Andreas. Not seeing him anywhere, she began backing toward the main part of the ship. "*Oma*, if we only have a couple of days left, I need to get to the Abbott & Costello movie that they are showing now. Please tell Andreas to look for me in the cinema."

"Now slow down, young lady," said Trollmann *Oma* as she grabbed Josie's coat sleeve. Smiling, Oma said, "You only know a few words of English. What difference will a couple more minutes make?"

"But they do the funniest things. I don't want to miss anything," Josie insisted. Pulling away from *Oma*'s grasp, she begged, "Please, *Oma*."

When *Oma* threw up her hands and waved her away, she ran as fast as her nine-year-old legs could carry her. As she rushed through the ship's door, she could hear *Oma* calling after her, "Save a seat for Andreas!"

A couple of days later, Josie and her small family stood huddled together on the deck of the *Queen Mary*. They welcomed the sight of land. Passengers began crowding around the railings as the massive ship pulled into the Port of New York at Ellis Island. She glanced at Trollmann *Oma*, *Mutter* and Andreas. *Mutter* looked very thin, but they each had on their best clothing for this special day. The ship blew its thunderous air horn, announcing their arrival. She pressed close to *Mutter* in hopes of shielding herself from the icy December wind. Suddenly the immigrants gasped in unison, causing Josie to look up. The huge statue of a woman looming in front of them amazed her. Tugging on Andreas's coat sleeve, she pointed ahead.

Her mouth dropped open. Josie could hardly believe what she was seeing. The lady was so majestic. "Andreas, what is that?"

Andreas didn't take his eyes away from the impressive figure. "She's called the Statue of Liberty. She is supposed to stand for freedom. One of the men playing shuffle board told me that France gave her to the United States as a gift many years ago."

"Some call her 'Mother of Exiles,'" a man leaning on the rail near them added.

"Oh!" was all Josie could say as she took in the beauty of the woman with the crown on her head, her right arm lifting a golden torch toward the sky. She was the most gorgeous blue-green that Josie had ever seen. She looked up to see *Mutter* and *Oma* crying. They were not the only ones.

Mutter reached for Josie's hand and put an arm around Andreas's shoulders. "Thank God, we are free!" She pulled them both close. "Thank God."

Josie cried too, but this time they were tears of joy. Then she laughed out loud as she took in the magnificent skyline of what would be her new country.

Everything seemed to be happening so fast, and very soon they were rumbling along on their way to California. As she sat on the bus Josie thought about the nice man with the curly brown hair. He had come from the American Embassy to meet them at Ellis Island and help them with what *Mutter* said was immigration paperwork and a visa.

Then he took them to a hotel to sleep before they began their journey to California. When he picked them up the next morning he made sure they had breakfast, but Trollmann *Oma* insisted he take them to a grocery store before their bus trip across the country. She wanted to be sure they all had bags of food to take with them.

"There will be restaurants and stores all along the way," the nice man had tried to reassure *Oma*. "There will be all sorts of places to eat near the bus stations."

Shaking her head, *Oma* said firmly, "What if the bus doesn't stop? Or, the restaurant isn't open? My *Kinder* are not going to go hungry!"

It was hard to remember how many days they had been riding in one bus or another, but they still had food. Smiling, Josie looked over at Andreas stuffing another piece of sausage in his mouth. "Give me some," she said, suddenly feeling hungry. "I want more cake, too."

Rolling his eyes, Andreas pulled a slice from the brown bag on his lap and tossed it at her. He said, "How many times does *Mutter* have to tell you that it isn't cake? It's called 'White Bread'!"

Josie didn't care what it was called; it was the best dessert that she had ever had. When her stomach was full she pressed her face against the cold window and watched power poles pass as the bus rolled by town after town. Many of the streets they traveled down had signs that read, "For Sale." Lifting her head up, she leaned across her sleeping mother and nudged her brother in the seat in front of them. Whispering, she asked, "Andreas, how do you pronounce S A L E?"

Turning to look at his sister, Andreas stretched. "I think that it's a woman's name. I heard a man at one of the bus stations call his wife 'Sally.'"

"Hmm," said Josie. "Who is this Sale who owns all of the properties we drive past?"

"I don't know, but she sure must be rich," Andreas said, rubbing his eyes as he turned back around and yawned. "There are sure a lot of signs that say, 'For Sale.'"

Josie leaned her soft curls back against the seat and pulled her coat collar up around her face. Sighing, she leaned closer to *Mutter* and reminded herself to ask Wurtz *Opa* if he had heard of a rich American woman named Sale. She must be very important to own so much land. *Opa* knows everything, she thought as the constant rolling of the bus wheels rhythmically moved Josie and her family closer to a new home.

CHAPTER 16

Fresno, California, Spring 1950

● ● ●

EVERYTHING WAS CONFUSING. A NEW country, a new language, a new school, and Josie missed Wurtz *Oma* and *Opa*. Thinking about them had made her throat tighten and her eyes well up with tears. Eventually a letter had arrived telling them that Wurtz *Oma* and *Opa* had arrived in the city of Fresno. They had found a little house not far from the ranch were her family had been living and *Opa* was going to help Andreas pick cotton. Josie had been so happy to see them again, but it was hard to say good bye when they went home.

Now, *Opa* and Andreas had new jobs and Josie was very excited about the changes. Trollmann *Oma*'s sister had given them a ride into town, and for the first time in months they were all going to live in the same place. Smiling from ear to ear, Josie reached across the crocheted tablecloth and patted *Opa*'s hand; suddenly she grabbed his large hand tightly with both of her small ones, as she didn't want to ever have to let it go. "*Opa*, I still can't believe that we get to live with you and *Oma* again. I have missed you so much!"

Standing up, *Opa* grinned as he snatched Josie up off of her chair. Wrapping his big arms tightly around her, he gave her a squeeze and looked directly into her bright brown eyes. "Believe it! We are all together in our new country. God willing, no one will separate us again." Dropping her gently to the kitchen floor, he stepped back and smiled. "What I can't believe is how grown up you are getting. I can hardly lift you anymore."

Wurtz *Oma* turned from the kitchen counter where she had been rolling the dough for fresh homemade noodles. "Josie, do you like America?" she asked.

"Sometimes I don't understand what my teachers are saying, but I'm making new friends. I like that part most of all. My best friend's name is Nancy." Josie giggled. "She's helping me learn English. Some of the kids make fun of how I pronounce words, but she doesn't laugh at me when I sound funny."

Walking across the room, *Opa* called Andreas and *Mutter* into the kitchen. Everyone was grinning as they gathered together in the small space. Clearing his throat, *Opa* got everyone's attention: "I have an idea. When Anna and I were in Southern California, Uncle Joe and Aunt Mary suggested that we take classes to learn English. I think they were right. It will help us find better jobs and we can help Josie with her studies." Putting his arm around Andreas's shoulder, he said, "Andreas, will you call the Adult School tomorrow to see if they have an evening class? We need something that starts after we are all home from work. You and I will be home from the bakery by noon, but your *Mutter* and Wurtz *Oma* won't be done cleaning houses until evening."

"Sure, *Opa*," replied Andreas, standing up a little taller. Josie wondered if he was trying to look important.

Shrugging, she peered around *Oma*. "Can I help cut the noodles?" Her mouth watered. "We haven't had home-made chicken noodle soup since we were in Glogon!"

"What!" exclaimed Wurtz *Oma*, wiping her flour covered hands on the bottom of her apron. "What has Trollmann *Oma*'s sister been feeding you on the cotton ranch?"

"Godal is a good cook, and she makes wonderful cook-ies." Josie smiled at the thought of the jam-filled cookies that Godal made. "But when we come home from working in the cotton fields everyone is too tired to cook or even eat much."

"Well," sighed Wurtz *Oma*. "Now that you are all go-ing to live in town with *Opa* and me that will not be a problem."

Josie felt sad for the first time since the reunion. "I wish Trollmann *Oma* was going to live with us, too," she said.

Wurtz *Oma* gave Josie a big hug. "We will all miss her, *Schatzie*, but she wants to spend time with her sister. Don't you worry, *Opa* will buy a car soon, and we will drive to the ranch to visit your Trollmann *Oma* often." Sliding a small step stool toward the stove, *Oma* handed Josie the noodles *and* let her drop them into the large pot. Josie was careful not to let the bubbling chicken broth splash up on either of them. The rich aroma filled the kitchen, and Josie's stomach gurgled in anticipation. As the family caught up on their time apart, *Oma* opened the oven door, and the fragrance of fresh homemade bread added to the celebration as she moved the large, golden loaves onto the shelf above the stove.

"Bring plates and bowls, Josie," *Mutter* said as she placed a dish of fresh, sweet butter on the table and smoothed the tablecloth's edges.

"I'm so hungry I could eat it all myself!" Josie declared.

"Am I hearing that you will not have room for apple strudel, *Schatzie?*" *Opa* laughed. "Andreas and I will be forced to eat your share."

Smirking, Andreas chimed in, "*Oma*, hide the strudel!" Sounding very serious, he added, "It's not safe to have it sitting that close to Josie." Even Josie laughed.

With moist eyes, *Opa* looked at each member of the family once again united around the table. God had been faithful, and there was enough food for everyone in this beautiful new land. Clearing his throat, he said, "Let's give thanks for being together for such a feast." Josie hoped that it would be a short prayer.

Epilogue

• • •

VATER (BORN FEBRUARY 20, 1913, in Los Angeles, California, while his parents were visiting family there)—After World War I, Frank Trollmann returned to Glogon with his parents to their farm. He was impressed into the Seventh SS Mountain Division, Prinz Eugen, of the German army during World War II. Andreas and Josie never saw their father again. As adults, they tried to search for information about him and went so far as hiring a detective, but without success. Many years later, at a Glogon reunion in Los Angeles, Andreas met a man who had been with *Vater* when he died (probably 1944). In a battle with Tito's Partisans in Yugoslavia, *Vater* stepped on a land mine and lost both of his feet in the explosion. The Partisans, who were on a hill above, rolled boulders down and crushed him.

Mutter (born December 10, 1914, in Glogon, Austro-Hungarian Empire)—Rosalia Wurtz married Frank Trollmann. After her escape from Yugoslavia, she moved to California with her family. She worked in the Fresno, California, cotton fields of the Stumphausers, who were relatives of Trollmann *Oma*. The Stumphausers had sponsored Trollmann *Oma*, *Mutter*, Andreas, and Josie in their immigration to the United States, and the family needed to work off that debt. After leaving the fields, she worked as a housekeeper in Fresno. Emotional problems eventually made it impossible for her to work, and she spent some time in a psychiatric hospital. As a result of all of the horrors that she and her family experienced, today she would most likely have been diagnosed as having post-traumatic stress disorder. Unfortunately, her symptoms were not widely understood by the mental health community at the time of her treatment, and she suffered further fear. *Mutter*, Andreas and Josie lived with Wurtz *Oma* and Wurtz *Opa*. *Mutter* attempted living independently for a while but eventually moved back in with Wurtz *Oma*. Finally, she had to be placed in a convalescent hospital. She died on June 21, 1980.

Trollmann *Oma* (born October 6, 1887, in Glogon, Austro-Hungarian Empire)—Ursula Buchler Trollmann moved to California in 1949. She lived for years with her sister, Godal Stumphauser, in Fresno, California. A few years prior to her death, she moved into a one-bedroom apartment across the alley from Josie and around the corner from Wurtz *Oma*. She died of a heart attack on July 21, 1967.

Wurtz *Oma* (born July 26, 1897 in Glogon, Austro-Hungarian Empire)—Anna Johs Wurtz moved with her husband, Johann, to Southern California, and later lived in Fresno, California with him until his death. Because of their daughter's mental health issues, Anna raised Josie. In the early '70s she moved in with Josie and her two great-granddaughters. Several years later she lived with Andreas and his wife, Ruby. She was in a convalescent hospital in Fresno at the time of her death on March 1, 1994.

Wurtz *Opa* (born July 17, 1900, in Glogon, Austro-Hungarian Empire)—Johann Wurtz moved with his wife to Southern California, near his brother-in-law and sister, Joseph and Mary Vidos. The Vidos family sponsored Johann and Anna's immigration to the United States. Later he and Anna were reunited with their daughter, Rosalia, and grandchildren in Fresno, California. Initially, he worked in the cotton fields with the rest of his family and was later employed at the Marigold Bakery, a German bakery in Fresno. He died of cancer in 1953.

Andreas (born August 14, 1932, in Glogon, Yugoslavia)—Andreas Trollmann moved to Fresno, California with his family. He enlisted in the US Army as a young man. He married three times, and had a daughter, Karen, with his second wife, Adelle. He and his third wife, Ruby, had a family business raising aquarium fish. Later, they owned house-painting businesses in Sacramento and Fresno. After Ruby's death, he moved to a retirement community in Clovis, California. He died in the hospital after surgery complications on September 16, 2010.

Josie (born April 10, 1940, in Glogon, Yugoslavia)—In 1949 Josie (Josefa) Trollmann moved to Fresno, California, with her family. Her first name was later Americanized and changed to Josephine and then shortened to Josie or Jo. Although she was old enough to attend the fourth grade at Sacred Heart, Josie was placed in a third grade classroom due to her language barriers. During that first year she met her lifelong friend, Nancy Moffa. In 1957 she dropped out of Roosevelt High School to marry a young rodeo cowboy, Herb Crouch. They divorced in 1967. She and Herb remarried in 1975, only to divorce a second time. They had two children, Susan and Cynthia. Josie eventually returned to night school to complete her high school diploma. Later, she went on to attend Fresno City College and became a registered nurse. Josie's daughter, Susan, and husband, Casey Lowe, had a son, Chris. Josie's daughter, Cindy, had three children. Her son, Deryck, and daughter, Robin, were born while Josie was living. Cindy's daughter, Apryl, was born after Josie's death. Josie died prematurely of a heart attack on August 11, 1994, in Fresno, California.

Yugoslavia

Yugoslavia was composed of six republics from 1946 to 1991. After Tito's death in 1980, Yugoslavia was again torn apart by ethnic strife. The republics of Slovenia, Croatia, and Macedonia declared their independence in 1991. Bosnia and Herzegovina withdrew in 1992. The two republics that remained, Montenegro and Serbia, then united as the Federal Republic of Yugoslavia. In 2003 the Federal Republic of Yugoslavia changed its name to Serbia and Montenegro. Three years later, in 2006, it split into two independent countries. So, the former Yugoslavia is now Slovenia, Croatia, Bosnia and Herzegovina, Serbia, Montenegro and Macedonia. Josie's little village of Glogon, Yugoslavia, is currently called Glogonj, Serbia. It is located a bit north of the Serbian capital of Belgrade.

Glossary of German Words

Frau—madam
Kinder—children
Liebling—beloved
Mutter—mother
Oma—grandma
Opa—grandpa
Schatzie—little treasure or sweetheart
Vater—father
Vertriebene—expellee or displaced person

Bibliography

The following adult sources were used in the research of this book:

De Zayas, Alfred-Maurice. *A Terrible Revenge, The Ethnic Cleansing of the East European Germans.* 2nd rev. ed. New York: Palgrave/Macmillan, 2006.

Hoeger Floss, Katherine. *A Pebble in My Shoe.* Palatine, IL: Pannonia Press, 2004.

Kopp, Hans. "The Chronicle of the Ungarlandische-Deutschen (Danube Swabians) in Hungary (Romania and Yugoslavia) and the German-American in the USA," *Landesverband der Donauschwaben, USA* (January 2008): 4–24. Accessed February 2008. http://donauschwaben-usa.org/chronicle-ungarlandische-deutschen.htm.

Kumm, Otto. *Prinz Eugen, The History of the 7th SS Mountain Division, Prinz Eugen.* Manitoba, Canada: J.J. Fedorowicy Publishing, Inc., 1995.

Neary, Brigitte, and Holle Schneider-Ricks. *Voices of Loss and Courage.* Rockland, ME: Picton Press, 2002.

Krutein, Eva. *Eva's War. A True Story of Survival.* Albuquerque, NM: Amador Publishers, 1990.

Koehler, Eva Eckert. *Seven Susannahs, Danube Swabian Societies of the United States and Canada.* n.p. 1976.

Tenz, Maria Horwath. *The Innocent Must Pay.* Bismark, ND: University of Mary Press, 1991.

Walter, Elizabeth B. *Barefoot in the Rubble.* Palatine, IL: Pannonia Press, 1997.

Wildmann, Georg, Sonleiter, Hans, Weber, Karl, et al. *Genocide of the Ethnic Germans in Yugoslavia, 1944–1948.* Lewiston, NY: The Danube Swabian Association of the USA, 2001.

Acknowledgements

● ● ●

First of all, we are deeply grateful to Josie Trollmann Crouch for the courage to share her painful memories of experiences in Yugoslavia during the years covered in this book. We are thankful to Andy (Andreas) Trollmann for sharing difficult memories of the trauma he shared with Josie and their family long ago. We appreciate so much the memories shared by John Trollmann, who also suffered through that time, answering countless questions, and for his generosity in validating the need for this book. Wenzel Tirheimer was generous in sharing many Glogon memories and answering questions. We thank the many people from the 2002 Glogon cousins' reunion for sharing valuable memories and encouragement.

We are thankful to other people who have led the way by telling their personal stories, and we think especially of

Maria Horwath-Tenz, Katherine Flotz, Elizabeth Walter, Glogon Cousins and the Danube Swabian Association of the USA.

We are grateful for those who have shared information, insight, or encouragement. Among these are Carl Hauser, Kathy Lara, Ray Borschowa, Uwe Morres, Susan Williams, Dave Dryer, Shelley Gregory, Erna Sesek, Dr. Tamas Cserfalvi, Helmut Tenz, Noelle Giesse, Dorel Vostinar, John Trollmann, Pat Long, Nancy Lewis, Ruxandra Meinze, John McClellan, Audrey Burger, Gabi Bugaisky, Rosina Schmidt, and Apryl Delp. This book is enriched because of their helpfulness.

Those who have patiently read and given helpful advice on improving the manuscript are Angelica Carpenter; Herb Crouch; Nancy Smith; Elizabeth and Madeline Fry; Cindy Sheheen; Vicki McGaw; Mary Lea Adkins; Michele McDaniel; Victoria McDaniel; Moses, Dinah, Zara, Johann, and Glory Glidden; Elizabeth Walter; Joan Reichling; Andrea Cheng; and Reverends George and Nancy Cushman, along with many others.

We are especially indebted to Dr. Carol Lilly, Dr. Alfred de Zayas, and Dr. Brigitte Neary for their expertise in this period of history, their generosity with their time, and their continued encouragement. They have helped in countless thoughtful ways.

We are grateful to Susan's son, Chris, for his support and understanding.

Special thanks go to Diane's husband, Doug Iverson, for his considerable editing skills, his patience, ongoing support, sense of humor, and willingness to cook dinner.

Endless thanks belong to Susan's husband, Casey Lowe, for encouragement and unending support during several years of a painfully slow writing process, for sharing the tears that were part of the process, and for patiently listening to multiple readings of difficult chapters.

Finally, we both thank God for having his hand on this project from the beginning, and for bringing us together in such a meaningful way.

Susan Lowe
Diane Iverson

Authors' Biographical Information

• • •

Susan Lowe is a licensed marriage and family therapist with an MS in counseling from CSU-Fresno. She has over twenty-four years' experience working with clients from multiple backgrounds, many which have been victims of trauma. In addition to maintaining a private practice, she has also taught courses at CSU-Fresno, Reedley College, and Madera Community College Center. She previously served as the behavioral health compliance officer for Fresno County. A first-generation American on her mother's side, Lowe lives with her husband, Casey, an accountant in California. Their adult son, Chris, also lives in California and has a bachelor's degree in bioengineering.

Diane Iverson has written and/or illustrated more than twenty books, primarily for children. She has served for fifteen years as the director of a service for homeless and low-income families and is a founding member of the Coalition for Compassion and Justice in Yavapai County, Arizona. Iverson lives in Arizona with her husband, Doug, a retired American literature and creative writing teacher. When the couple is not enjoying time with their two daughters and seven grandchildren, they volunteer for various Christian, environmental, and charitable organizations.

Made in the USA
Charleston, SC
26 January 2016